JESS FULLER

Echoes of Fate

Woven Fates Book 1

Contents

EDITOR SHOUT OUT

This book has been edited by Eden House Books.
You can find them on Facebook.

COVER DESIGNER SHOUT OUT

THE COVER OF THIS BOOK WAS DONE BY
WYNTER DESIGNS BOOK COVERS.
YOU CAN FIND HER ON FACEBOOK.

DEDICATION

To the people who want to give up, NEVER stop fighting.

TRIGGER WARNINGS

- HARM TO CHILDREN (WITHIN THE PROLOGUE AND CHAPTER 1).
- OPEN DOOR SPICE PRESENT IN CHAPTER 18.
- VIOLENCE.
- GORE.
- BLOOD.
- DEATH OF PARENTS.

THE MAP OF CRAYTON

I made this map myself using a map bundle that I bought from Etsy. The map bundle is by Lizard Ink Design. I completed it with Procreate.

It is just so readers have a general idea of where everything is. It's not perfectly accurate, as I only had one page to work with. But it lets you see roughly where everything is in the book that's mentioned.

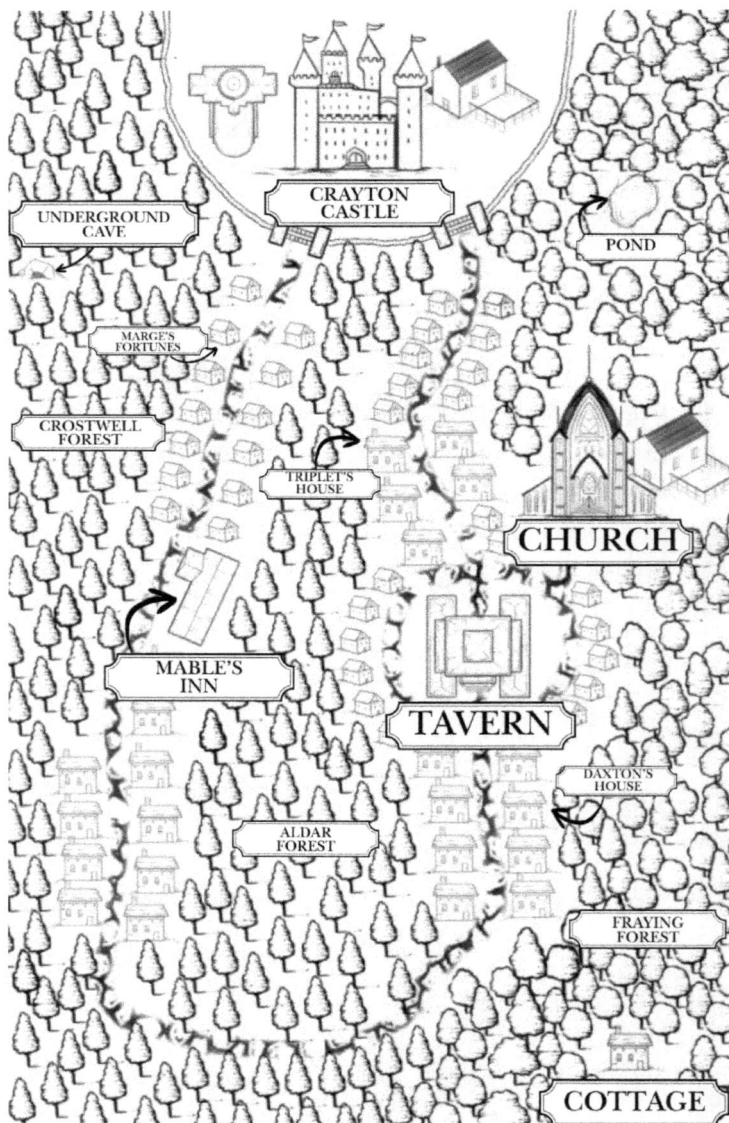

UNDERGROUND CAVE

CRAYTON CASTLE

POND

MARGE'S FORTUNES

CROSTWELL FOREST

TRIPLET'S HOUSE

CHURCH

MABLE'S INN

TAVERN

DAXTON'S HOUSE

ALDAR FOREST

FRAYING FOREST

COTTAGE

PROLOGUE

FENRIS

Logan and I were patrolling around the outskirts of Hayselwood, our cosy little town within the kingdom of Crayton. We had been out most of the night and other than the scurrying of wildlife there was no action, no movements. This was how it was most nights, which we were usually thankful for. But I craved the kill of a demon. It was a rush to exterminate them and know I was protecting our kingdom from such evil.

Whenever demons were around they wreaked havoc. Leaving destruction everywhere they went and killing innocent people. It's the whole reason I became a Witch Hunter in the first place. To help people and try to rid the world of as many demons as I could.

We'd get asked often why we were called Witch Hunters when

we fought more than just witches. The truth was, we started out only hunting witches until more and more creatures needed to be disposed of.

"Let's head in for the night, Fen. It's almost morning." Logan patted me on the shoulder and I nodded.

We made our way towards the church where all Witch Hunters resided.

I rubbed my eyes and yawned. Being out all night always took its toll on me.

The streets were blanketed in utter darkness. It was just before dawn and the cold air brushed against my skin. I squinted and saw Andras coming into view, one of our fellow Witch Hunters. He stopped in front of us and put his hands on his knees, panting. His brow was drawn tight and sweat trickled down his face.

"Andras, what is it?" Logan asked.

Logan, the leader of the Witch Hunters, and my best friend, took his duty to all of us very seriously. Despite being only twenty two years old – he was the youngest of us – he had been the best choice to take over when the previous leader died from heart failure.

"A filthy witch just killed my scholar! I shot the witch dead but she comes from a coven," Andras spat once he had finally caught his breath.

I gaped at him. My guts were churning, the way Andras spoke always made my skin crawl.

"Give me a full report, Andras," Logan commanded.

"I was out patrolling with my scholar. Next thing I know we're being attacked by a witch. She knocked me to the ground while she strangled my scholar. I shot her but it was too late." His face was pained and close to tears but something about it didn't feel right. He never treated the scholars with enough dignity to use their names. I had always found it odd.

"Take us to the scene," Logan said.

"I'll take you. But after that I want that coven exterminated. Every last one of them dead. We must act fast before they find out what we did. We have the element of surprise."

My eyebrows furrowed. What did he mean by 'before they find out what we did'? We didn't do anything. The way he said it made my stomach drop. "What exactly did 'we' do?" I asked, suspicion evident in my tone.

Andras appeared taken aback and hesitated a moment. "They'll want revenge on us for killing one of their own, even if it was in self defence. They'll be coming for us if we don't act fast."

He was still acting weird but I noted it for a later discussion with Logan. Right now we had to deal with what was at hand, the dead witch and scholar.

"How will we even find them?" I asked.

"I know where they are. The dumb witch didn't realise she'd left a trail," Andras replied.

Another thing that struck me as odd. Why would a witch be so careless? It was unlike them to not cover their tracks. They had always used their magic to ward people off so they couldn't be found.

"Let's go inspect the scene and investigate the coven after," Logan said, but he glanced towards me with suspicion in his eyes.

***

I had to turn away from the bloodied, lifeless bodies of the two women. Seeing them lying there made my mouth feel dry and my head feel dizzy. I hated seeing anyone hurt but children and women had always been a particularly hard thing for me to witness. It was as he described. The scholar, Bianca, was on the ground with another woman, the witch, on top of her. She had a bullet wound to the head, blood and brain on the ground meshing with the dirt. It was already coagulating.

"You see what she caused? We need to go now," Andras pushed.

"Let me gather more men. We're going to need numbers to take on a full coven," Logan said.

Andras tapped his foot on the ground. "Fine. Meet me at the pond north of the church."

"Take Fenris with you. I won't be long." Logan left before I could say anything.

We walked together in silence towards the pond. Andras was one of those Witch Hunters that mostly kept to himself. Did a great job, but didn't make friends. Nobody really knew him that well. He joined us five years ago and had helped us get rid of many demons and witches, but he wasn't someone I ever went out of my way to talk to or spend time with.

On the other hand, Logan and I had been with the Witch Hunters since we were young, growing up in the castle we were given a choice between Royal Guard or Witch Hunters. Logan was born for this but I chose this path because it felt like the one that helped more people.

"I'm sorry about Bianca. That must have been hard to see." I tried my hand at making small talk.

He shrugged. "It's all part of the job isn't it? We win some and we lose some. People will lose their lives, that's inevitable. We just have to try and make sure it isn't us."

His words sent a shiver down my spine. I didn't know how to reply so I stayed silent as we continued to walk.

When we finally got to the pond I sat on a nearby rock while Andras scouted the area. Not long after we arrived, Logan and over a dozen Witch Hunters came into view.

"Lead the way, Andras," Logan said stiffly.

We moved quietly throughout the Herring Forest, located to the east of Crayton. Logan and I trailed right behind Andras, the other Witch Hunters behind us. It was thankfully still night time, the sun hadn't even peaked over the horizon yet.

As we made our way through the thick trees, we came towards a clearing. Logan stopped the other Witch Hunters with a hand in the air before gesturing Andras and I to follow him closer. A sense of dread was building in my chest the closer I got, an overwhelming amount of fear. I felt a prickling sensation moving down to the base of my spine and a cold sweat against my neck. These feelings were hard to ignore, they made me want to turn and run. As Witch Hunters we knew better. We recognised the feelings, we had been taught to lean into them instead of shy away.

A ward was here. This was where the witches would be.

Andras removed his dagger from his belt, the runes etched into the hilt glowing softly in the night. He waved it back and forth in front of the clearing, his runes beginning to glow brighter. I looked down, noticing he held his branding iron tightly in his hand by his side. He was the only one of us who had one. It made me anxious, but Logan allowed it. He would brand witches after killing them to show he was the one who had defeated them, like some sick game.

Once we knew where the wards were, Andras knelt down and stabbed his runed dagger into the ground. Oddly, he also smashed his branding iron on the ground next to it. As he did, it glowed a vibrant red. The dagger was how we broke the wards but I wasn't sure what he was doing with his branding iron. A light began to spread out along the ground from both the dagger and the branding iron, crawling further and further, the usual gold glow was laced with red. I felt the immense pressure building in my ears that would always occur when wards were collapsing.

Finally, an invisible curtain rippled and fell to the ground, exposing twelve cottages. Smoke billowing from their chimneys and lights turned off, there was no movement within the village. They should have been alerted by the ward dropping by now and rushing out, so why weren't they?

I looked towards Andras and he was smiling. It must have been something to do with that red glow that was emitted when he used the branding iron.

"What was that red laced with the gold, Andras?" Logan asked.

"Why aren't the witches coming after us?" I added.

"Just a little something I've picked up along the way. We must hurry before they stir." Andras put his branding iron back in his belt but held onto his dagger.

"You will explain to me later, Andras. This tool could be useful to Witch Hunters," Logan said and Andras nodded.

My stomach turned, I didn't feel good about this. About any of it. Yes, they were witches but there would be women and children. Men, taking care of their family. We were about to murder them in cold blood while they slept.

"Logan, I don't know about this," I whispered so Andras wouldn't hear.

"Don't fret, Fen. It'll be fine. This is what we're trained to do," Logan answered.

He misunderstood my words. I wasn't frightened for us. I was frightened for them.

"Men, infiltrate their homes quietly and dispose of them quickly. If you let them awaken, the battle will be harder. They will use their magic on you," Logan whispered to everyone.

We all moved in unison toward the cottages. Logan and I followed Andras towards the bigger cottage. This must have been the leader of the coven's home. I swallowed, forcing down the knot in my throat.

Andras silently opened the door and we made our way inside, tip toeing to avoid creaky floor boards.

The cottage was homely. It had a kitchen to the left and the fireplace and chairs to the right, the warmth from the fire giving us a moment of relief from the cold outside. Towards the back of the cottage there were three doors.

We moved carefully towards them. Andras opened the middle door and found a bathroom with nobody inside. Logan opened the left door which opened up into the main bedroom. A woman was sleeping in the bed peacefully. I took a step back, but Andras didn't falter. He walked right in, unsheathed his sword from his back and as he did the woman stirred. She glanced up at him as he plunged the sword deep into her chest. She gurgled on her own blood before becoming lifeless, eyes wide with fear and shock. The cloying scent of witch blood coated my nostrils, an earthy, slightly bitter scent of freshly dug dirt.

I placed my hand over my nose. We turned to go to the remaining room, but as we did I jumped when I saw a young girl standing there. She couldn't have been more than ten years old.

"Who are you?" she asked, rubbing her eyes.

"Your death," Andras replied.

The girl started to back away towards her bedroom.

"Logan, she's a child," I choked out.

Logan hesitated for a moment before finally saying "She will grow into an evil witch, Fen. We can't allow that." Logan's eyes narrowed and a sick feeling punched me in the stomach.

I couldn't watch this. I ran out the door and immediately threw up as I heard the screams of that little girl.

What were we doing?

CHAPTER 1

MARELLA

A s I peered through the trees at the stars in the night sky I wished, if only for a moment, that my life wasn't filled with demons and being hunted. I sometimes caught myself longing for a normal, human life. One where my parents were still alive and I didn't have to hide from the world. Maybe I'd own a bookshop and be married to a baker's son with little children running around everywhere. A normal, uninteresting life.

In this lifetime, that wasn't the case. I was born a witch and I'd die a witch. The only good that came from my magic was the ability to help people. To exterminate the demon filth that plagued our world. They'd infiltrate Earth and possess or kill us. Humans or witches, they didn't care. Although, demons and witches had one thing in common. We had to be careful and hide in the shadows because the Witch Hunters were ruthless towards both our kinds.

They called themselves Witch Hunters but they hunted so much more than just witches. I assumed they came up with the title since it wouldn't have rolled off the tongue as easily to include everything. Figures the witches would get the short end of the stick.

I had been hunting one specific demon for a couple of days now. Tracking its kills throughout the forests and trailing its scent. It was lurking in the trees between the small town of Hayselwood, and the Crayton castle walls. Stalking a demon in this area was always tricky, because the trees were thick and housed spiderwebs and it was rampant with wildlife. It certainly made good hiding spots for them. Disturbing a hooting owl, or interrupting the night time hunt of a speedy, almost invisible to the eye fox, was a sure-fire way to alert this slippery demon to my presence. I had to be careful and quiet. Something my mother would remind me of constantly... back when she was alive anyway.

Children in Hayselwood were going missing and I heard rumours among the gossiping townsfolk that these children were being found days later in this very area. Nothing but husks remaining. Their bodies devoid of everything inside of them, hollowed out.

I picked up a grey feather and turned it around. It was evident this was a Scree Demon. This particular demon had the ability to glimpse future events. I hadn't seen one with my own eyes, but I'd read about them and had seen pictures in the town library.

I stepped carefully between the trees, listening to every moving sound. Whenever I heard a branch crack or an animal scurry it made my hairs stand on end.

I was starting to get bored and wondered if I would even find the demon tonight. Where was it? Surely it was close by. I decided I wouldn't leave until I found it and killed it. I was so sick of hearing about the poor children who were being slaughtered. The Witch Hunters were also clearly having a hard time finding it too otherwise we wouldn't still be hearing about children going missing.

It was then I heard a shrill scream. A child's scream. My heart raced.

"Somebody help me," the child sobbed.

I darted through the trees in the direction of the sound, skidding to a sudden stop when there, only a few feet away, was the demon. It had the child - a little girl - held above it. She was terrified and had blood running down her arm.

The demon was small with a hunched back and long, feathered wings. It reminded me of a bird with its beak and long, black talons. From the side I could just make out those milky white eyes. Even though the Scree demon could see future events, it was completely blind. They relied on their other senses and glimpses of the future to see the world around them. Its long tail was whipping around on the ground like a lion's. The Scree Demon was ferocious and tension prickled along my shoulder blades at the sight. It appeared as terrifying as the pictures in the books. The demon used a long, black talon to scratch the little girl's face before licking her cheek.

"Let her go right now!" I screamed as I got closer.

It whipped its head to the right and opened its beak wide, a piercing screech bursting out. Its blind eyes stared right at me. My heart thundered faster and I tried to calm myself so it wouldn't smell my fear. It dropped the girl to the ground, and she cried out as she stumbled away, running back towards Hayselwood.

The wind picked up, flicking my curly brown ponytail against my cheeks. I stifled my nerves, knowing the demon could smell what I was in the wind.

"Well, well what do we have here?" the demon screeched as it sniffed the air.

"You've made my night. I have been itching for a fight." I was mustering a confidence I didn't feel, and hoping it'd fall for it.

I held my sword firmly in my sweaty palm. It was a longsword with a black hilt that once belonged to my father. The memory of it laying on the ground, abandoned after he died, flitted through my mind, forcing me to take a breath in to refocus.

The demon crawled along the ground, using its front talons to pull itself towards me. The sight of it made me shudder. I felt its milky white eyes staring deep into my soul.

"Silly witch. I've killed hundreds of your kind. What makes you any different from all the others?"

"I don't know. I guess we'll find out once your head is severed and your body is burning," I said with a smile.

The demon lunged at me then and I swiftly moved to my left. It stumbled, turning as it let out a blood curdling sound, like nails on stone. Its talons glistened in the moonlight as it tried to swipe at me, but it missed and caught them on a tree beside me. I had just enough room to duck down and as I did, I brought my sword up into the demon's stomach. The demon let out a shriek of pain, flailing around. I kicked it back as I removed my sword from its stomach, black blood spraying out of the open wound.

"You stupid little witch. I'll kill you," it snarled, holding its stomach with one hand, and using the talons on its other hand to bring itself back to its feet.

"I feel like I have the upper hand here but okay," I chuckled, taunting the demon.

It snarled at me as it bared its teeth, and it once again lunged at me, no longer caring about the wound in its stomach. This time its bloody hand wrapped around my arm, and I screamed in pain as its talons pierced into me.

"What were you saying?" it taunted, those eyes staring blindly right into mine.

I could see the reflection of my green eyes in its milky white ones. It was so close that I could smell the stench of its breath on my face.

A loud bang echoed. Like someone shot a pistol, back in the direction of Hayselwood. That was all I needed.

It lost focus for a split second as it gazed towards where the sound came from. I used that as an opportunity to push the Scree demon to the ground and began summoning a ball of fire to launch at it. Its eyes started glowing and as my fire reached it, the demon's eyes shot out a radiant light that connected with my fire. The power of it blasted us both back and onto the ground. The world blurred and I coughed as my lungs struggled for air.

I opened my eyes, but I wasn't in the forest with the demon anymore. I was in my cottage, but the images were blurry. I could see a figure, even blurry I could tell it was the Demon Queen, Lilith by her shape and that flowing, fiery red hair that was pictured in my mother's grimoire. There was a figure standing near me and another one closer to Lilith but I couldn't make out who they were. Lilith's blurred figure hurled what looked like a sword towards me and then I saw black.

I was brought back to the present, where the demon was on the ground, screeching in pain. I picked up my sword that had fallen on the ground and lunged at the demon. It plummeted right into its chest, and it stopped moving.

"What the hell was that?" I said to myself out loud, breathing heavily from the mix of fear and adrenaline.

But as my breathing slowed and my thoughts came back to the present moment, I knew exactly what that was. A vision of my death, forced on me unintentionally by the demon.

***

I sat next to the demon for what felt like hours before finally removing my sword from its chest. I hacked at its neck until its head fell limply to the ground and I summoned my fire magic once more. I let the fire dance in my hand before throwing a ball of it at the demon. It went up in flames and the stench burnt my nostrils, making my eyes water. As I stared down at the burning demon, the wound on my arm made itself known. I glanced down, feeling the sting as blood dripped, soaking the arm of my white shirt. I pulled out a bandage from my pocket, thankful I thought to take it with me, and wrapped it around my arm, tying it off as best I could. I had to get home before I got caught. I wasn't in any shape to fight anyone else. I had to be quick, there were so many things that roamed around at night. It wasn't just demons I was worried about. I just hoped the girl had gotten back to town safely.

I got to my feet and sheathed my sword, walking the way I had originally come. Back to my home and back to Hulda where she would be waiting to hear about what took place tonight.

I was thankful Hulda raised me. She had taught me all I knew about my magic. Because of her healing magic she could easily heal this wound of mine. I, unfortunately, didn't possess the kind of magic needed to heal bigger wounds. Give me a cut and I could heal that with ease but anything bigger was beyond me. I was more powerful in other ways. Fire was my biggest weapon, and I could wield it with ease. Not many witches could control fire so I did feel lucky.

Leaves crunched to the left of me. Someone was following me. I kept walking, pretending I didn't notice it but keeping myself aware and ready to run. A shadow fell over me, my heart racing, and then a voice spoke.

"Marella, it's been a while." I knew that voice all too well.

I turned to face Andras, a Witch Hunter who had tried and failed to kill me on several occasions. He had the upper hand now with my injury unfortunately.

He was wearing his usual black leather outfit with his black, flowing cloak. His floppy, black hat was beginning to fade to a greyish colour from overuse. I knew he was bald underneath the hat from a previous fight we'd had. I snickered quietly at the memory of him running after his hat and it blowing away in the wind while I made my escape.

Those big, black boots crunched on the ground as he moved closer. He had a pistol and a dagger attached to his belt. Next to the dagger was his branding iron. I had seen the witches he'd killed and branded with it. I would make sure he'd never be able to use that thing on me.

As he moved slightly, the black hilt of his sword appeared just above his shoulder, strapped to his back.

"What, no greeting?" he pouted.

"It hasn't been long enough, Andras. Can we do this another time, perhaps?" I asked, trying not to give attention to the wound on my arm that was still stinging.

I was hoping he would think the blood was someone else's. I had to try and avoid this confrontation somehow and get home to Hulda. At least I knew I wouldn't die tonight. That had to be some comical intervention.

Andras removed his pistol and angled it towards me.

"Guess not." I rolled my eyes. This was so inconvenient.

"It almost feels bittersweet to kill you now. Oh well." Andras smiled as he cocked his pistol.

His shot went wide and his pistol clattered to the ground as he lurched to the side, shoved off balance by another figure.

Was that another Witch Hunter?

He was wearing a similar outfit to Andras. He wore a black mask with a big hat, so I couldn't see who he was or what he looked like. Weird that a Witch Hunter was attacking his own, but I wasn't going to argue. They both unsheathed their swords and started swinging at each other, clanging as loud as a shot from a pistol sounded around the street. Their movements were both smooth and evenly matched.

"Run," the other Witch Hunter said to me as he pinned Andras to the ground.

I was about to do just that when Andras kneed the Witch Hunter in the stomach. I flinched, struggling with whether to jump in and save the person who was saving me or run like he told me to.

Andras went to grab for his dagger but pulled out his branding iron instead. My eyes widened as Andras slashed at the Witch Hunter and hit his hand that he was using to cover his face. He screamed out in pain and managed to roll away before being hit with it again. I felt frozen in place, fighting with myself about what to do.

"Run, now!" he yelled out again.

I didn't need him to say it a third time. It was all I needed to be pulled out of my struggle. I ran all the way back home, my lungs burning when I finally collapsed at my front door.

CHAPTER 2

MARELLA

"A Witch Hunter attacking another Witch Hunter? How odd," Hulda said as she poured pancake batter into a pan. The smell hit me instantly and my gut answered with a growl.

Hulda had healed my arm last night and sent me off to bed without much conversation. She knew I needed to rest, and that I'd explain the events of the night before to her when I wasn't so drained.

I told her everything the moment I woke and found her in the kitchen. Well, almost everything. I wasn't about to tell her that I had a vision of my death. I didn't want her to worry any more than she already did.

"I didn't even see the Witch Hunter's face. He wore a mask that completely covered it," I explained.

I set the table with plates, knives, and forks before taking a seat.

Hulda turned to face me with a spatula still in her hand.

She brushed her fingers through her short, blonde hair and sighed. "Maybe you should take it easy for a while, Marella. Lie low just in case this other Witch Hunter decides to hunt you as well."

I'd obviously made the right choice not telling her about the vision.

"I can't sit around while demons continue to ruin lives. While Lilith continues to send her minions to Earth. Witch Hunters aren't going to stop me."

Hulda grunted and turned around to flip a pancake. There was silence for a moment before she finally spoke. "I just hate you going out there by yourself. I especially hate seeing you come home hurt."

"I can take care of myself. You taught me well, Hulda."

She crossed her arms and her lips thinned.

I sighed in resignation, rolling my eyes. "I promise I'll try to be more careful. I'll stick to the shadows instead of walking in the middle of the streets."

Her arms fell to her side. "Fine. I can't stop you but just... be careful." She started plating up the food and took a seat across from me.

She handed me the plate of pancakes and I shovelled some on my own plate, drowning them in syrup.

"I have a couple of people to tend to in town and would like you to come with me to get in more practice," Hulda said, changing the subject.

"Sounds good to me. I'll take any opportunity for healing practice. Although I don't think I'll ever be as good as you." I started digging into my food.

"Remember, Marella, we all have our talents. Healing may not come naturally to you, but fire does. I wish I could wield fire as well as you do."

Hulda tried to summon fire in her fingertips but only got a flicker.

"Fire may be useful, but healing would be more so. You're lucky, Hulda."

She placed her hand upon mine and smiled. "We are both equally lucky with the power we were gifted. Each is useful for different things."

"I know, I know." I rolled my eyes and smiled back.

Hulda swatted my hand for rolling my eyes at her and we laughed. Moments like this made me forget about demons and Witch Hunters, if only for a moment. Wishing it was just us two and we were normal people living close to everyone else, interacting with other normal human beings.

After finishing breakfast and cleaning up we both grabbed our supplies and robes. We had to be careful when going into town, so the Witch Hunters didn't catch us. We still had no idea how Witch Hunters could pick out witches from regular people.

The hooded robes we wore kept us from being noticed and thankfully didn't stand out since everyone seemed to wear them to protect themselves from the dusty roads around Hayselwood.

I wore my dark brown hair in a high ponytail. This was my go-to hairstyle as it kept everything neat and away from my face. Hulda didn't have to worry about such things since her hair was shoulder length.

As we walked in silence towards the town, I couldn't help

but ponder the night before. Knowing I was going to die and soon was going to eat away at me. I could feel my future self when I was in that vision. I felt how young I still was, and I felt the terror. I could feel my heart racing beneath my chest and I felt my worry. I was only twenty three years old now, was I the same age in that vision? Would it happen before my twenty-fourth birthday? I only hoped that I was going to be the only one to die that night. I knew I would have to tell Hulda eventually so she could plan an escape.

Thinking of Hulda having to see Lilith again brought forth memories of the night my parents died. Memories of blood and death. A shiver went down my spine as I remembered how much blood there was on the forest floor. My father's lifeless body next to his sword with his eyes still open and looking in the direction of where a pool of blood was with no body. We assumed my mother tried to escape but was taken away by animals. The whole scene would always be seared into my brain. I shook the thoughts away before more crept in. I wasn't sure I'd ever be ready to let them fully materialise.

When we finally reached Hayselwood we stopped for a moment to scan the town for Witch Hunters.

Hayselwood was a big, beautiful town. There were a number of houses lining the streets. Within the centre of the town was where all the markets and shops were huddled together. The tavern was a big building right in the middle of all the shops and the market stalls were scattered around the circle it created. There were also more houses and shops leading up to the gate that opened up to Crayton Castle.

"I can't see any out at the moment so we should be okay for now," Hulda said as she glanced around.

Her face was always tight with nerves whenever we entered

27

the town, but healing people was important to her, it was ingrained into her and was a massive part of who she was, so she still went anyway.

"Where are we going first?" I asked as we continued through the streets.

"I thought we could continue practising with smaller wounds. We can go see Walter first. He has a small cut along his thigh," Hulda explained.

Walter was an older gentleman who was constantly getting himself hurt so Hulda knew him well. He farmed crops outside of town so the machinery he used was always giving him trouble.

When we arrived at his house, Hulda knocked on the brown, wooden door. Beatrice, Walter's wife, answered before she could even finish knocking.

"Hi Hulda. He's at the dining table. I told him he wasn't allowed to move about everywhere until you came." Beatrice gestured for us to enter.

"Walter, how are you? What happened?" Hulda placed her hands on her hips.

I stood next to her, rubbing my palms together. I always felt anxious when I was the one about to heal.

"Same as usual. Damn machinery cut my leg when I tried to climb into it. I swear I'm cursed," Walter replied, taking a drink of what smelt like alcohol.

"Well, I have Ella here with me today so she's going to heal you if that's alright." Hulda placed a hand on his back.

Walter peered at me and back to Hulda. "That's quite alright. I just want to get it done so I can get back to work."

Hulda nodded and gestured for me to take a seat next to him. I focused and did what Hulda had always taught me. I placed both my hands on opposite sides of the cut and breathed in and out, calming my thoughts and sending energy down to my hands and into the wound. Sweat trickled down my face and there was a tingling sensation within my hands from straining to perform magic with an ability I wasn't paired with. It took a while but finally, gritting my teeth to the point of pain, I opened my eyes as the heat in my veins cooled, letting me know the wound was healed. I gazed up at Hulda grinning and she nodded, a smile crossing her face.

"Wonderful. Thank you, dear," Walter said, getting to his feet.

He grabbed his jacket that was hanging by the front door and left. Beatrice, who was in the kitchen area the whole time, came out and handed Hulda a bag of coins.

"No doubt we will see you again soon with how he's going." Beatrice shook her head as she opened her front door. "Thank you again. We do really appreciate you always coming out to use your gifts. I know how dangerous it is for you."

"Of course. What is the point of having such a gift if we don't use it? You have a good day, Beatrice and let me know if you need me again."

"You mean when Walter needs you again." She huffed a laugh.

Hulda laughed along with her as we headed out of the house. A quick scan of the streets again and we were on our way to the next house.

We were out for most of the day going house to house healing people who had sent word for Hulda's aid. I only healed two more small wounds after Walter since the rest required more advanced magic.

When we finally finished for the day, the sun was setting, and my feet were killing me. The tavern was buzzing with people and laughter as we passed it on our way home.

"You did well today, Ella," Hulda said as we moved carefully through town.

"Thank you, I appreciate that." I smiled at her.

I pulled my hood over my face and lowered my head as I saw three Witch Hunters moving through the streets.

The feeling of constant seclusion always got to me, always having to ensure we were careful whenever we ventured into town. I could count the number of times on my hand that I had even been inside the tavern.

Not many of the townsfolk knew we were witches. We had a select few Hulda trusted like Beatrice and Walter and that's mostly because Hulda said she had known Beatrice since she was a young girl. Some of them were suspicious but didn't dare speak out against us. They'd stare at us or grab their children and run off. I didn't understand the constant hate for our kind. Okay, sure, there were a few bad witches out there that gave us all a terrible name but I could say the same for humans as well.

Hulda grabbed my arm and pulled me closer to her. I smiled at her and squeezed her arm as we kept walking. Her praise and affection always made me feel like I could do anything. Exactly how I always believed my mother would have acted. It simultaneously warmed and cooled my heart, knowing that I was lucky enough to have such a woman in my life, and sad for the life I could have had with my parents.

We were halfway to our cottage when Hulda stopped suddenly.

"Want to practise something a bit different?" she asked.

I gave her a confused look since nobody was around us that needed healing. She crouched down and touched a flower that looked like it had seen better days. Within seconds the flower's stem grew straighter, its wilted petals unfurling and its beautiful purple colour returning from the pale grey it was before. The flower went from looking like death to this beautiful, healthy purple flower.

"The Earth needs healing too sometimes." She gestured for me to try on a flower close to the one she had just healed.

I crouched beside her and cupped the flower in my hand. Closing my eyes like I had done several times before, I focused my breathing and energy. Hulda gasped and I opened my eyes to find flames engulfing the petals. I got to my feet and moved away as I watched the flower turn to ash and the flame burn out.

"Wow, I can't even bring a flower back to life."

"There may be some things you will never be able to heal no matter how much you train. Just like I'll probably never be able to wield fire like you. But it doesn't hurt to keep trying and to give those abilities a stretch every now and then."

I sighed at her words. I should be thankful for my fire magic, and I was, I really was. But I often wondered if I could heal as well as Hulda, would I have been able to heal my parents that night? Would I have been able to get to my father in time and find my mother in time to heal them both? But that just made me remember all the blood and I gulped, knowing there was no saving them from that.

"Stop it. I know what you're thinking and there was nothing you could have done, Ella. I couldn't have even healed them," Hulda said, wrapping her arm around mine.

I opened my mouth to reply, but snapped it shut when movement caught my eyes deep in the trees.

"Did you see that?" I asked Hulda as I dropped her arm and

skulked into the trees.

"Ella, it's getting late. We should get home," she whispered desperately as she caught up to me.

I didn't listen to her as I continued forward. I positioned myself behind a tree with Hulda beside me. Peering around the trunk, within the clearing ahead were several figures.

"Your sacrifice won't go unnoticed, girl. The demons will be glad to have the soul of a scholar," a slimy voice murmured.

I took a hurried head count. Five males, all dressed in black robes.

Demon worshipers.

These despicable cretins sacrificed people to the demons and sometimes, although very rarely, they'd be granted simple powers. They craved it. The girl they had surrounded trembled as they closed in on her. She had her long, sandy blonde hair in a messy braid and was wearing a white dress that was now dirtied.

I jumped at the sudden sound of the shrill alarm I knew as that of the Witch Hunters. The alarm was always so deafening.

"Ella, we have to go," Hulda whispered to me.

Panic was all over her face.

If we left right now we could get home before the Witch Hunters arrived. But the girl would die and it was something I refused to let happen.

"The Witch Hunters won't get here in time to save this girl. I can't just leave her here."

One of the men grabbed her by the arm and the girl cried out. I leaped out from behind the tree and towards the men.

"You need to let her go right now!" I scowled.

The man let go of the girl's arm and moved towards me, leering. He pulled out a dagger from his belt but before he could use it, I summoned my fire and threw it at him. The fireball exploded against his shoulder, burning through his robes and searing his skin. His eyes widened as he held his shoulder and screamed, his dagger dropping to the ground. He thrashed about wildly to put the remaining fire out. Hulda snuck up behind one of the men closest to her. She kicked the back of his knee and as he fell down she grabbed the dagger from his hands and hit him over the head with the hilt. He hit the floor instantly. The remaining three men surrounded me and as I whirled around, I saw the girl rummaging through her satchel.

"Nowhere to go now, little witch," one of the men sneered.

Hulda looked on in a panic, she knew she wouldn't be able to take on three men. I could see her mind working, trying to come up with a plan to take them together. As the men came closer, I chanced a glimpse again at Hulda who was looking at the girl.

"Use your fire!" the girl yelled as she threw something into the air.

I didn't have time to think as I summoned my fire and threw it into the air. It connected with the dark sand like texture she had thrown. I quickly dropped to the ground, covering my head with my arms. There was a loud noise that made my ears ring, and my body was thrown forcefully against a tree, the pain reverberating up my spine.

"Ella are you okay?" I could just make out Hulda's voice above the ringing in my ears.

I coughed from the impact. It felt like my bones were broken but I was alive and didn't appear to have any open wounds. I glanced around until my eyes landed on Hulda, she was unscathed.

33

"I think so," I finally managed to rasp out, my voice starting to feel hoarse. I got to my feet and held my side where it felt like my ribs had been crushed.

"I am so sorry." The girl came running towards me, worry written all over her face.

"What was that?" I asked.

"Gunpowder. I didn't expect it to create such a blast."

The girl gestured at the destruction, the three men had been blasted away but they didn't fare as well as I did. They were strewn about in opposite directions, their bodies mangled from the impact and their faces blistered with burns. If it wasn't for my immunity to fire, that would have been me on the ground.

"Woah," I mumbled, horror stealing any other words I might have said.

"The alarms. They've stopped," Hulda's voice was shaking. "We have to go now, Ella."

"Come with us?" I urgently asked the girl.

She nodded and as we began running towards our cottage I asked "What's your name?"

"I'm Greta," she answered, puffing.

"I'm Marella and this is Hulda." I pointed in front of me.

We came to an abrupt halt, running right into Hulda. "What's going on?" I asked her.

I looked up and saw a dozen Witch Hunters coming straight for us.

CHAPTER 3

FENRIS

I was walking through the town when I heard a commotion towards the trees near the Castle walls. Someone screamed and I started to sprint. As I got closer I placed my back firmly against a building and peered into the trees. I could just make out a girl fighting what appeared to be a Scree Demon. The demon grabbed her arm as blood trailed down, dripping on the ground.

I panicked and grabbed one of my pistols out of my belt. Before I could think too hard about it, I shot the side of a building. The demon gazed in my direction. The girl didn't lose focus and it was then I saw what she was. My eyes widened as she threw a fireball at the demon at the same time it threw its powers towards her.

She was a witch. I had aided a witch.

I stumbled as I raced to get away. I couldn't believe what I had just done. If Logan ever found out I had helped a witch I'd be in big trouble. I had to get away as far as I could and hope she didn't see me when I made that shot.

When I felt like I was a good enough distance away, I stopped and leaned against a building to catch my breath. I pinched the bridge of my nose. Why had I just left her there? Why hadn't I eradicated her like a Witch Hunter was supposed to do? Maybe I should go back and do just that. I shook my head to rid myself of such thoughts. No, I knew I couldn't kill her, someone so innocent looking.

I wandered around for a while, stuck in my thoughts, trying to focus on my nightly patrol of the town and not think about what I had just witnessed.

As I walked along the streets I noticed Andras standing in the middle of the road.

"It almost feels bittersweet to kill you now. Oh well." I heard him say.

I peered further and saw the witch from earlier, standing there with her arm bleeding even more so than before. She appeared pale.

Andras was just about to shoot her with his pistol and I wasn't sure what came over me in that moment but I ran and tackled him to the ground.

"Run!" I called to the mystery girl as I pinned Andras down.

We struggled and fumbled around then Andras grabbed his branding iron and slammed it into my hand. I groaned as the pain vibrated through my hand, the heat of it instantly blistering my palm.

I glanced over for a split second to see the girl was still there. "Run, now!" I yelled and finally, she listened.

I punched Andras in the face while he was watching her run away and I got to my feet. "Logan isn't going to be happy when he hears you injured one of his best men," I said as I held my hand close to my chest.

"I don't think Logan will be happy to learn his best friend and most trusted Witch Hunter saved a horrid witch." He spat on the ground at my feet.

"Fine. I agree not to say anything if you won't," I answered through gritted teeth.

"Fine. But just so you know I will kill that filthy witch." He made to leave then turned back to face me. "You might want to get that hand looked at before the blisters become unmanageable." He smirked and I fought the urge to punch him again.

I spent the rest of the night trying to track the witch to no avail. Wherever she lived, it was well guarded with magic and wasn't in town as I came across no wards.

When I finally got to my room I sat at my desk and pulled out a piece of paper and pen to begin writing my report. My desk was positioned in front of my fireplace which I was thankful for as I reached my fingers out to the flames, toasting off the chill of the night.

The reports were sometimes frustrating to write but they were necessary. Having access to reports dating back generations was essential for us to understand our enemy. Understand why we did this.

I finished writing them then removed my hunting attire and hopped into bed, thinking of the interesting witch I happened upon. How her brown ponytail swayed in the wind and strands caught against her pink lips. How she moved with such strength but also grace. How she hesitated, if only for a moment, when I told her to run. Was she contemplating helping me? A Witch Hunter? My eyes fell closed as I drifted off.

***

There was a loud knock on the door, jolting me awake, immediately putting my feet on the ground. Logan entered before I had time to answer.

"Where is last night's report, Fenris?" Logan asked with his authoritative voice.

"What time is it?" I rubbed my eyes.

"Time for you to get up," he answered, crossing his arms. "It's after lunch."

I suppressed a smirk at his tone. Logan and I grew up together in the same household and were like brothers. In the three years since the previous Head Witch Hunter Daxton had died of old age and Logan was appointed to take over at just nineteen years old, we'd managed to rid the world of more demons than ever. Logan took more risks than Daxton, who was more interested in preserving our dwindling numbers rather than helping the people we were trained to protect. I stood by Logan's choices and knew he wanted the best for Crayton.

We hadn't come up against many witches though, they were more elusive. Daxton swore he went up against a coven of them once by himself. Twelve witches, he said. I found it hard to believe but he swore black and blue that he managed to defeat them all when he took them unawares. I guess we'd never truly know.

My thoughts flickered to the coven we took care of not long ago and it made me feel sick all over again. I pushed the memory from my mind.

"Well?" Logan tapped his foot on the ground.

"Apologies, Logan. I got caught up with... something. I have them on my desk ready for you to sign off on," I answered, rubbing my hand over my face.

He moved over to the desk and took a seat, signing the papers without even reading them.

"Are you ready to head out?" he asked, handing me the signed report.

"Sounds good to me. Let me run this report to the scholars and I'll meet you outside."

Logan and I walked out the door and went opposite ways.

I headed towards the library where the scholars kept their reports stored. I handed it over to a girl named Sandra. She stamped it once she saw Logan's signature then walked away with it to store it for future keepings.

I left the library and headed towards the entrance of the church to Logan waiting on the stairs. He was seated on the top stair looking out into the town. The town that he was sworn to protect from other worldly creatures and I knew he was proud of his duty. By the positioning of the sun I could tell it was already afternoon. I had slept most of the day away which always happened when my patrols were at night.

He saw me and got to his feet. "Ready to go?" he asked.

"I am keen to sleep in my comfier bed that's for sure," I joked.

Logan and I were the only Witch Hunters who lived some-where other than the church. We had our own rooms in the church when we needed to stay there but when we weren't at the church we resided at the castle.

We headed towards the stables together to the west. The

church was the biggest building in the small town. It was almost as big as the castle to accommodate all of the Witch Hunters, scholars, priests, nuns and the nave. Witch Hunters and scholars took up the right wing of the church and the priests and nuns took up the left wing with the nave being directly in the centre.

"Heading out, sir?" the stable hand, Geoff, asked Logan while he brushed the mane of a chestnut horse.

"We are off to the castle. Do you have two horses already saddled, Geoff?" Logan asked, patting the horse.

"Dallas is in the back and has saddled a couple for the day." Geoff gestured towards the back area of the stable. Logan nodded and we headed inside.

"Logan! Fenris! How are you?" Dallas, a gangly boy of almost nine, squealed.

He'd been working for Geoff, his father, since he turned six, and he still got excited to see us every time we crossed paths.

"Just catching the bad guys, making sure the town is safe. How is school?" I asked, leaning against a wooden post, the hay at my feet crunching under my boots.

"Good. My writing is getting better. I'll have to show you next time I see you," Dallas beamed.

"We can't wait to see it." Logan patted him on the back.

"You can take Rhino and Fred. They are ready to go." Dallas pointed towards two dark brown horses that were already saddled up.

We led them outside before mounting them and heading along the path towards the castle, the hooves of the horses beating along in rhythm with each other.

As we rode through the streets of Hayselwood I thought it would be a good time to see what Logan knew about witches.

Maybe he knew more than we did after taking over as Head Witch Hunter.

"I had a dream last night and it got me thinking," I started and he glanced over. "I was wondering if you knew any more about witches since taking over Daxton as our leader?"

He looked at me quizzically. "Are you planning to seek out some witches any time soon, Fen?" he asked.

I laughed nervously, "Nothing like that. I was just curious. In my dream we were fighting them together so I just wanted to learn more." I lied to him through my teeth and though I felt bad, I needed to know more.

"I only know as much as you. That witches are all evil and should be destroyed just like demons. That they are much harder to find. Which is why we haven't come across them as often as demons," he answered.

"Do you think we will ever find more?" I asked.

"I'm sure we will eventually but right now our focus is on the enemies we can find. Demons. If we ever come across more witches though, we have the training to destroy them."

I didn't like how he said it. Like they weren't people. Because that girl seemed just like a normal human being to me. Maybe we were wrong? Or maybe they were just good at concealing their evil side, part of their ability to hide among us.

We rode for a while longer in silence, taking in the beautiful day around us, until finally coming to a stop at the castle gates and the guards opened them immediately. Seeing us almost every day we never had to share who we were.

When we finally reached the castle stairs, it was late afternoon. The castle stable boys took Rhino and Fred from us as we dismounted and led them away.

As we walked the fifty or so steps to the top I admired the ivy covering the building and the gargoyles positioned evenly on either side of the top of the stairs.

Upon entering, I took in the beautiful main lobby with a flowing, curved set of black marble stairs on either side leading up to the next floor. No matter how long I lived here I'd always admire the beauty of the castle.

"I don't know about you but I'm starving," Logan said, rubbing his stomach.

"I could eat. Let's go harass Imogen in the kitchen. See what she's got for us," I said, a smirk crossing my face as we walked to the back of the castle towards the kitchen.

"You two are going to clear me out before dinner," Imogen scolded us half an hour later. "Always hanging around like a pair of bad smells, gobbling pies faster than I can get them out of the oven." She shook her head in disapproval.

"It's really your own fault for being such a good cook." I gave her a winning smile and she stopped working for a moment to roll her eyes at me and sigh.

"These meat pies are amazing, Imy." Logan tried buttering her up.

"Call me Imy again and I'll throttle you," she replied, pointing a rolling pin in his face.

Logan put his hands up in a defensive stance and chuckled. We always felt like kids again around her.

"Come on, you two can get out of the kitchen now. You're taking up valuable space." Imogen started shooing us out into the hallway.

"We'll be back later," I called out.

"I don't doubt it," she called back.

"I'm sure she's going to kill us one of these days," Logan laughed.

"She wouldn't be able to live without us though," I replied as we ventured back into the main lobby.

I peered out the big, glass windows on either side of the main double door, the sun was just beginning to set. It was glowing and leaving a beautiful pink hue along the skyline.

"You two were annoying Imogen again, weren't you?" I turned and watched as Lyra descended the black, marble staircase to the right.

She was wearing a long, flowing black dress adorned with gold embroidery which brought out her hazel eyes, the sleeves flaring down with the dress. Her wavy, blonde hair was bobbing past her hips as she walked. She had always been like a sister to me although not to Logan. He had always been infatuated with her but she didn't return those feelings.

I didn't know much about my past, but I was thankful everyday that King Aldric took me in when I was young and allowed me the opportunity to become a Witch Hunter, working beside Logan and inviting me to become a part of his family.

"Princess Lyra, your dress is exquisite." Logan's head dipped in a shy bow.

He couldn't keep his eyes off her. She blushed and nodded her head in thanks as she reached the last step.

"Caught anything lately?" she asked, referring to witches, demons, and demon worshippers, clearly not feelings.

I laughed in my head at the joke I told myself regarding Logan's feelings towards her.

"Nothing worth mentioning," Logan answered and then added. "How about you? I heard King Aldric was organising a party for your birthday soon?"

"He's always looking for an excuse to have a party. I'm only turning nineteen. I don't see the reason for the fuss." She shrugged her shoulders.

"Hey, I wish someone threw me a party for my nineteenth," I exclaimed.

"You wouldn't be saying that if your parties still had apple-bobbing and the court jester clowning for us," she said, and we all shared a laugh.

A sudden noise tore through the castle as the doors were wrenched open. Standing in front of us was Billy, another Witch Hunter, panting.

"What's wrong?" Logan asked as Billy tried to catch his breath.

"Demon worshippers have been spotted outside Hayselwood within the woods. Someone from town was walking along and saw it. She came straight to the church. The woman said there was a girl matching Greta's description," Billy explained, still huffing.

Logan cursed and we both started sprinting towards the door, but Lyra grabbed my arm.

"Could you stay, Fen? I need to talk to you. It's important," she asked in her sweetly coated honey voice.

Logan glanced back and nodded before running out of the castle towards the stables.

CHAPTER 4

MARELLA

B locking our escape, the Witch Hunters took in the massacre of five males surrounding us three women. I wiped my sweaty palms against my clothes and tried to breathe deep through the hammering in my chest. Thankfully though, unless fate decided to randomly change itself for this moment, I knew I wasn't going to die right now. No, that would come later. I knew we had to think of something and fast because there was no way we could take on twelve Witch Hunters. I looked over to Greta, wondering if she was going to tell them we were witches. Before I could say anything, the Witch Hunter at the front started talking.

"Greta, what happened? Are you hurt?" He came towards her and checked her over.

I held my breath in a panic.

"I'm fine, Logan. These women saved me." Greta pointed at a satchel on the ground. "These women went through their satchel while they were distracted with me. They found a grenade and used it."

I let out a silent sigh of relief. Hopefully she sounded convincing enough. It did look like a grenade had gone off in the area.

"Thank you." Logan looked towards Hulda and I with a look of gratitude painted on his face.

There was something about him. He didn't seem as dark as Andras was. Speaking of Andras, I was just beginning to thank my lucky stars he wasn't among the Witch Hunters when he emerged from the bushes to the left as if he was summoned by my very thoughts. I pulled the hood over my head and tried to cover my face as best I could.

"Andras, where were you? Greta was attacked by demon worshippers, and she was assigned to you. We don't want to lose yet another scholar," Logan demanded.

He was obviously the leader. Andras huffed in anger, but his expression quickly changed to something more neutral.

"My deepest apologies to you, Greta. I was finishing up my report for the Scree demon I extinguished outside the castle walls, I had no idea it would take so long," Andras explained.

That prick just took credit for my kill. I wanted to choke him, but I knew I couldn't show my face. I couldn't risk him speaking up and telling the other Witch Hunters I was a witch.

I saw Andras from the corner of my eyes as he glanced at Hulda, who he thankfully hadn't met before, then looked at me. He moved his head to try and get a look under my hood and my heart started thumping in my chest.

"Well, is the report done?" Logan asked, drawing Andras'

attention back to him. I let out a silent sigh of relief.

"Oh, yes, of course. It's waiting for you on your desk," Andras tripped over his words.

"Can I escort you anywhere?" Logan asked.

"I was actually thinking of taking them to the tavern, to share my thanks," Greta piped in.

"I have to head home but you two should go ahead," Hulda said.

"Are you sure I can't escort you?" Logan asked one more time.

"No, that's alright. Thank you. It's not that far away and what are the odds of being attacked a second time." She gave a nervous laugh.

"Okay, well, if you're sure. Thank you again," Logan said.

Andras was talking to one of the younger Witch Hunters, whispering to each other. I couldn't make out what they were saying but I was glad he was distracted.

The other Witch Hunters began cleaning up the mess around us. Hulda gave me a hug and started walking in the direction of our cottage and I followed Greta back towards town. I could hear Logan giving orders to the Witch Hunters as we walked away. I was thankful to leave quickly, worried they'd find out what I was.

When we got to the tavern the sun had completely set and the night sky was filled with bright, twinkling stars. A half crescent moon could be seen just over the church. A shiver went down my spine seeing that building.

As I hadn't been to the tavern often I stopped to take it in. The outside was tattered with paint chipping and an old sign.

Greta looked over to me. "Is everything alright?"

I sighed. "I just haven't had a chance to take in the town

before."

Greta looped her arm around mine. "Let's change that then."

We both entered the tavern and I somehow felt safe with this woman I had just met, free to be able to be here and not worry about what could happen. I guess if she wanted to she could have had me killed but she didn't. I was interested to find out why a scholar kept my secret. Even though we saved her life it still felt odd.

"Pete, can we grab two ales and keep them coming?" Greta called over the loud crowd as we approached the counter.

As we waited for our drinks I glanced around. It was sizable and well kept. It could easily fit a large number of people. The bar area was positioned in the middle of the building where it was arranged in the shape of a circle, wrapping around, and giving the bar maids more area to work on the counter tops. There were two entrances to get into the tavern, one on either side. To the left and right of the building there were roughly ten stairs that led down into foyer areas that housed six sets of wooden tables and chairs for customers. There were wooden bar stools around the entire bar, which I assumed we'd be sitting at but once we got our ales, Greta led us away down into the left foyer. We took our seats at a secluded table, and I took a large gulp, thankful for the liquid to wet my parched throat.

"Why didn't you tell them I was a witch?" I said softly, getting straight to the point.

She tightened her grip on her glass and appeared shocked for a moment that I'd asked. "You saved my life. Besides, I'm not sure if I can trust the Witch Hunters anymore."

I had to stop my mouth from falling open. Witch Hunters and scholars had been working together for decades, if not centuries. The fact that a scholar was saying they couldn't be trusted was alarming.

"I know we just met but that has to be the last thing I ever expected you to say to me." I huffed a nervous laugh as I took another sip of ale, trying to hide the alarmed look that I knew was written all over my face.

Of course, the thought was crossing my mind that this could very well be a trap. Being that Andras was her Witch Hunter, it definitely made me feel more cautious. But again, Greta seemed different from the rest of them, she seemed pure and honest.

"Look, I know you have no reason to trust me. But I will keep your secret from the Witch Hunters. They don't need to know you're a witch," she whispered the last word, looking around to make sure nobody heard.

There was thankfully nobody too close to us, they were all mostly towards the centre of the tavern.

I sighed as she lifted her ale to her lips. I decided to take the plunge and give her the benefit of the doubt. I only hoped I wasn't going to regret it, that my intuition was correct.

"Okay, you said you can't trust the Witch Hunters anymore. Why?" I asked.

"I didn't say I can't. I said I wasn't sure if I could or not."

"Fair enough." I waited for her to answer as she paused for a moment.

"I haven't always been Andras' scholar. Bianca, the scholar we lost recently, was partnered with Andras, until she was murdered."

"Wait. Murdered?" This time I couldn't stop my mouth from falling open.

"In cold blood. She wasn't killed by a demon, a witch, or a

demon worshipper. In fact, I know exactly who killed her and why."

"This is why you aren't sure you can trust the Witch Hunters?" I asked, shocked at what she was so readily revealing to me.

She downed the rest of her ale and slammed the glass on the table, her fingers shaking as they came to rest on the table. She was scared.

"So, who killed her?" I asked carefully.

"It was Andras. He found out I knew and tried to have me killed as well. That's why I was by myself surrounded by demon worshippers. That bastard must have tipped them off somehow to get me out of the way so I wouldn't talk. I still haven't figured out if he acted alone but that's why I'm not sure whether it's only him I can not trust."

"I've had a few encounters with Andras and know how cruel he is. This news, as disgusting as it is, doesn't surprise me when it comes to him."

"You've had more than one run in with Andras and lived? Wow... you must be a powerful witch, he's ruthless." She was shocked but I shrugged at that.

"So, why did he kill her?" I leant my arms on the table and held my cup of ale tightly in both hands.

"Andras captured a witch and the scholar worked with that witch in the tunnels under the church. She worked day and night for him and was able to make his branding iron. She came up with a way to always have it hot and ready. "

"There are tunnels under the church?" I interrupted her, surprised it never crossed my mind. Of course, they had tunnels at their disposal.

She nodded her head. "The tunnels lead to all different areas of the town, including one entrance into the library of the castle. If you aren't familiar with the layout, it can be a bit of a maze down there."

"What happened to the witch?" My blood began to boil because I knew the answer that was coming.

"I have... suspicions that Andras may have killed her."

I pinched the bridge of my nose with my fingers, feeling a headache coming on. I had to find a way to permanently get rid of him. He was really a thorn in my side.

"What made you suspect him?" I sighed.

"Andras has always rubbed me the wrong way, from the moment I met him. He's a slimy, horrid man. I started following him around when I finished training to become a scholar. He never noticed the shy, new girl. At least he didn't notice me until recently," she sighed. "I always wondered how his branding iron was able to stay hot all the time. I figured it surely had to be a witch, what else could it be?" She paused and fiddled with her fingers on the table. "The same night the scholar was found dead, a witch was also found dead. He told Logan the witch killed the scholar, and he shot the witch. That sealed the deal for me that Andras was up to something and he may have killed them because of it. It was all too coincidental."

"What are you going to do?" I asked.

"Maybe I can talk to Logan. I think he is just about the only one who possibly can be trusted, but I'm not sure I'm prepared to risk my life on it." She rubbed her temples with her fingers.

A bar maid came towards us with two new glasses of ale and removed our empty glasses. I was thankful for the drink given all the information I was taking in.

"You can't go back there if Andras wants you dead," I said matter of factly.

I know I just met Greta, but I felt protective of her. I didn't want to see her hurt; I could tell she was a good person. She lied for me, on the chance that I could have seriously hurt her, or worse. There weren't many people out there that would risk everything for a witch.

"Unfortunately, I can't just disappear. Scholars are tied to the church, and the Witch Hunters. I'd be hunted and brought right back," she sighed.

"You need to tell someone. You said Logan may be the only one who can be trusted. Can you try and feel him out? Drop hints?"

"Maybe. I'll think about it. If I'm wrong about Logan, they'll just get rid of me too." She covered her face with her hands in frustration.

I took a second to think. I just saved this girl, and she was trusting me with all this information. I couldn't let anything happen to her after all that. But how was I supposed to protect her when I couldn't even enter the church and she couldn't run away? This feeling of impotence was the worst thing about being the kind of person who always wanted to help others.

"If you need to get away you can come stay with me. Just... be careful. Come back here in a couple of nights and I'll be waiting to make sure you're okay. If you don't come, I promise to come find you." I rested my hand on top of hers for comfort.

"Thank you. I don't know why you're helping me, but I appreciate it."

"It's what I do. I help people. Besides, you saved my hide today," I said with a chuckle.

"Maybe the Witch Hunters need to change their views and work with some of the witches."

I laughed a little. "That'll never happen, trust me. They hate us."

Greta frowned at my remark. "They've been taught to hate your kind for a very long time. But lessons can be untaught if one is willing to learn something new."

I crossed my arms. "Can I ask why you're so receptive to me? To my kind?"

"Why wouldn't I be? You saved my life when you could have let me die, too. That's all I need to know about the kind of person you are." Greta drank the rest of her ale.

I stretched my arms into the air. "I better get home before Hulda starts to worry too much. Don't forget... two nights. I'll meet you here."

"I won't forget. Thank you, Marella."

"Call me Ella."

"Thank you, Ella." She smiled and got to her feet, giving a nod before walking out.

CHAPTER 5

FENRIS

"L et's go," Lyra said as she led me to my room within the castle.

"Why are we going to my room?" I asked.

"What I have to say can absolutely not be overheard," she answered as she dragged me inside and closed the door.

Lyra wandered in further then sat on the brown fabric lounge that was facing my fireplace. I walked towards the window looking out into the castle grounds, the workers in the gardens were packing up for the day. I turned back around so I was facing Lyra, who was now looking at her fingernails.

My room at the castle was somewhat like my room at the church but much bigger. My bed was double the size and much softer in this room. The red satin sheets and blankets were much better than the scratchy white sheets at the church.

"I need you to keep an open mind and hear me out, Fen. You're one of the very few people I trust with my life." She had her serious face on, so I knew I had to match her tone.

"Lyra, what's going on?" I furrowed my eyebrows.

"I have never told anyone this before, but I have spies in Valdori. They are back in Hayselwood and sent a letter for me to meet with them urgently. I'm taking George and I want you to come too."

George was a royal guard specifically assigned to Lyra. He had been by her side since she was just a baby.

"How long have you had spies for?" I was curious, and a little affronted that she hadn't told me.

She crossed her arms. "It's a recent development. Their cousin is a cook here and introduced me to them. She told me they were stealthy."

"Why do you need spies in Valdori? What's going on?"

"I hope nothing, but I suppose we will find out tonight."

"Does the King know you have these spies?" I clasped my hands behind my back.

"Define know?" Lyra squinted suspiciously.

I sighed. "You'll have to tell him eventually, Lyra. Especially if it's something big that you discover."

"I will, I will. Stop being pushy and mature." She stuck her finger in her mouth and made a vomiting gesture.

I ignored her smart remark. "When is this meeting taking place?"

"Tonight. We need to leave soon before it gets too dark. We can take the tunnels through the library."

She got up off the lounge and paced towards me, stopping near the window, and looking up at me with a pleading look in her eyes.

"I don't know, Lyra. If something happens to you and the King finds out, he'll skin me alive."

She laughed at that. "My father dotes on you more than me, you'll be fine."

"How did you get George to agree to this?"

"George agreed to do this for me because I wouldn't take no for an answer and he cares for me like a daughter. He knows I'd just try to go alone."

I brushed my fingers through my hair out of anxiousness and frustration. She knew if she asked me with no time to spare, I wouldn't be able to refuse her. I had to go with her otherwise she'd go without me and if something happened to her, I wouldn't be able to forgive myself.

I grunted. "Fine. But you need to stay close to me. If anything happens to George or I, you run, understood?"

"Understood." She motioned across my room to the bed-room door. "I'm going to go dress in something a bit more ... running friendly just in case. I'll meet you at the library in an hour."

I nodded, and she walked out of the room. What was I getting myself into? These spies of hers better have useful information for the trouble we were about to go through, for the trouble the Princess was about to go through.

***

"Well, I guess we aren't taking the tunnels," Lyra said an hour later as we stood in front of the library's entrance. King Aldric was standing right there talking to some of his guards.

"Guess not," I answered with annoyance.

"George, dear. Can you get a carriage ready? We want to

leave in five minutes."

George nodded and walked off. I snapped my head to the left and glared at her with a shocked expression.

"I must advise against going out this late at night, Lyra. Too many things can go wrong."

"I have George and you, what more protection could I possibly need. It'll be fine, Fen. You worry too much." She walked off towards the castle's entrance without another word. I reluctantly followed.

A few short minutes later, the three of us jumped into the carriage and made our way to Hayselwood. I gazed out the window for the entire trip, focusing on anything that could be lurking out there and staying silent.

Lyra talked to George about some gossip within the castle and must have known I was focusing because she didn't try to talk to me.

When we finally arrived, the sun was almost completely set, and I was beginning to panic that this wasn't such a good idea, and I should have tried to convince her to stay in the castle. Maybe I could have gone in her place. A silly thought because I knew she would never let me when she could just go herself.

"Are we ready?" Lyra asked, looking at George then me.

"Let's just make this quick and get back to the castle," I answered as George nodded his agreement. He was a man of many words, our George.

We climbed out of the carriage and were met with a two storey brick house. Thankfully, it was situated closer to the castle than the church. As we approached the beautiful dark timber door, I scoped the windows on either side. On the second floor, a woman peered out one of the windows at us.

"Come on, let's get inside." Lyra placed her hand on my back and pushed me, gesturing me to move.

The person who answered and led us into the living room was a younger man with black, curly hair and a pipe in his mouth.

"Thank you for coming, Princess," he said directly to Lyra.

Two more men entered, and my eyebrows shot up. I shook my head, disoriented because I was seeing three of the same person. Lyra saw my expression and giggled. George must have appeared the same because her eyes fell on him and her body shook with laughter before gesturing to the three men that looked alike.

"They are triplets, you buffoons. They make for very good spies. Not only because of their skills but because looking the same has come in handy for them on several occasions. This is Theodore, Adrian, and Glen." She pointed at each triplet as she said their names.

"I'm not Theo, he is!" one of the men pointed at the other and they burst out laughing.

"Stop it you three," Lyra said, using an authoritative tone but smiling through her teeth.

"Who is the woman upstairs?" I asked.

"That's Magnus. She's our mother," Adrian answered as Lyra, George and I took a seat on a big, dark blue lounge.

Lyra took on a more serious tone. "Is it as bad as we expected?" she asked.

"Worse," Theodore said as he sat on the chair opposite us.

Adrian and Glen stayed standing in the walkway, glancing around like they were listening out. "It's not just a war with a small group from Valdori, it's the kingdom itself. King Neldor wants to take Crayton for himself, and he plans to eradicate the whole kingdom to do it," Theodore explained.

I couldn't believe what I was hearing. We always had our

suspicions that King Neldor wanted to destroy Crayton, but this was huge news. What were we going to do? How were we going to protect the kingdom from a potential war? Did the King even know about this or was he in the dark like the rest of us?

"How is that possible? He must have something at his disposal, another way to secure his victory. Something we don't know about. There is no way he can win a war against us with numbers alone. We're evenly matched," I said, hoping they learnt more.

"It's possible, but we don't know for sure. We plan to travel back tomorrow morning and continue our investigations on the matter. We thought it important that you know this as soon as possible, Princess," Theodore said and Glen added "We have no idea when they want to attack so we wanted to make sure you got the information. At least now you can prepare. Hopefully we can get more intel for you."

Lyra gave Glen a smile. "You three have never let me or your kingdom down. We are grateful for your loyalty. See that you are properly fed tonight and make sure you all get plenty of rest. Be careful out there. Any sign of trouble and you all come back, I don't want any of you getting hurt." Lyra nodded at George, and he handed Theodore a big brown leather pouch full of clinking coins.

"We will send word when we return again," Theodore said, getting up out of his chair, signalling the meeting was finished.

I glanced out the window to see night had fallen, the stars high in the sky and the half crest moon between them. My main focus was now getting Lyra back to the castle in one piece. I was thankful in that moment that I had George with us as well. He was a damn good fighter. I'd seen him in training several times and he was near unmatched.

"Until next time, princess Lyra," Glen said, moving out of the way so we could pass.

I looked cautiously all around as we walked out the front door. The streets were always pretty deserted at night for fear of lurking demons. There would usually be a couple of Witch Hunters out and about surveying the area to make sure all was clear but there didn't seem to be any close by.

I rushed Lyra into the carriage that was hidden behind some bushes, George was close behind.

"We need to get you back to the castle right now," I whispered as we all sat inside and shut the door.

"The castle isn't far away. I'm sure we'll be fine." Lyra leaned her chin on her hand and gazed out into the night. "Such a beautiful night. I wish we could enjoy it and walk the streets right now," she exhaled.

The castle gates came into view and I let out a sigh of relief, my shoulders relaxing from the built up tension.

I glanced over at Lyra and replied. "Don't even think about..." but that feeling of solace was short-lived as I heard a roar outside the carriage. "Get down now!" I yelled as I pushed Lyra to the carriage floor.

Just as I placed myself over her, I glanced out the window and saw a large, angry demon barrelling towards us with its red, glowing eyes and big, black horns. It crashed into us and as the carriage toppled over I felt pain radiating through my skull before the world went black.

CHAPTER 6

MARELLA

After finishing the rest of my ale, I walked out of the tavern and immediately hugged my arms close to protect myself from the cold, fresh air. I needed to hurry up and get back to Hulda before she worried too much. After what happened with those men, she would be counting the minutes until I got home.

As I started to walk away, my shoulder was slammed into by a man frantically trying to get to another group of men.

"There's a demon close by. We saw bodies," I overheard the man explaining through panting.

I immediately ran over to them and wrenched him around to look at me.

"Where's the demon?" I asked.

He glared at me like I was crazy. "You best be getting home, miss. Don't trouble yourself. Can one of us escort you?" The man patted my upper arm.

"Thank you, but no. Can you tell me where you saw the bodies?" I tried again.

As I spoke, two Witch Hunters strode purposefully by. I hoped the men wouldn't notice otherwise they'd go to them and I'd lose the chance to kill this demon myself. I kept my eyes on the Witch Hunters but kept my focus on the man. My heart raced from the need to get to these demons before they did.

He hesitated like he was thinking about whether or not he should tell me but finally he said, "that way." and pointed past the tavern, towards the castle.

I thanked him as I watched the Witch Hunters talking to some other bystander who was making several arm movements. They appeared more annoyed than anything.

I fell into a run towards the danger. As I circled around the tavern to make my way towards the demon, I tripped over a bloody, mangled body. He was no longer moving and I quickly crawled away, getting to my feet.

What was going on?

At least I knew I was heading in the right direction, but I needed to hurry before something like this happened to anyone else.

I broke into a run again, following a long trail of bodies, suddenly skidding to a halt when I heard a pained groan. I stopped and peered around then noticed a man roll over, clutching his stomach, blood flowing freely from an open wound. I urgently ran towards him and helped him into a sitting position, causing him to hiss in pain.

"What happened?" I asked, panic rising in my throat.

"Demons." He coughed up some blood. "Three of them. They came out of nowhere and started attacking." he hissed again as he clutched his stomach harder.

"I'm so sorry this has happened to you." My eyes burned as tears started to form, and I choked on a sob.

"Please ma'am. Just go save yourself." His eyes fluttered and then he went still.

I wiped the tears from my eyes, got to my feet and sprinted in the direction he had indicated. My heart shattered for these people as I continued to pass dead bodies. Why weren't the Witch Hunters patrolling this area? Or had they already done a round before these attacks occurred? If that was the case, I knew I had to be quick incase they came around soon, especially after seeing those two Witch Hunters in front of the tavern.

I careened around a corner and came to a halt, dashing into a hiding spot between a cake shop and a bookstore. There were Witch Hunters fighting off three demons that looked like Freegle demons and were twice the size of the men. They were gigantic with pale blue skin and long pointy ears. Quickly recalling what I had learnt about such demons, I remembered that they possessed the ability to drain a victim of their energy with a single touch. I would need to be careful not to get too close.

I peered around and noticed the scholars were off to the side hiding behind a building, they all appeared terrified but were writing on their wax tablets. I assumed they were taking notes of the fight. It struck me how dangerous the life of a scholar was, and my thoughts roamed to Greta being in the midst of a fight like this, whether she would even survive to see one with all she knew of Andras.

I got distracted from the whole reason I was here as I returned to watch the fight, how the Witch Hunters moved. They were a sight to behold, I had to admit. They were fast and strong, dodging the demons with grace and vigour. They eventually took one down and one of them set the demon on fire while the other Witch Hunters took on the other two demons. I tried to catch the faces of the men but didn't see anyone I recognised. Not Andras, Logan or that mystery Witch Hunter who saved my life. I wondered where he was?

They finally took the second one down with a runed sword, glowing gold in the darkness of the night, and I prayed they'd be done soon so I could leave. The fight was blocking every potential exit. I was trapped until they cleared out. I couldn't turn back the way I came because some of the scholars had moved from their hiding spot and were now blocking that path, and I couldn't move forward because they would see me. I couldn't see any way around them which was frustrating. If they saw me and I lingered around them too long they would find out I was a witch and most definitely kill me right after they finished with those demons.

The Witch Hunters took down the last one then started to walk away. I was confused why they weren't setting the other two demons on fire to ensure they were definitely dead.

The answer to my question was made clear when I watched the scholars walk towards them and start collecting samples. They cautiously cut off some of their skin, swabbed saliva from their mouths and cut off some of those sharp claws.

I whispered 'finally' to myself when they set the demons on fire.

It was always a relief when the job was done permanently, three more demons that would no longer be terrorising the people of our town.

They watched the flames eat away the flesh of the demons, before sauntering away towards the direction of the dead bodies I had come across earlier. I let out a sigh of relief that I hadn't been seen. I was annoyed I didn't get the glory of fighting the demons, but I would have been outmatched anyway.

I was leaving my hiding spot and about to race home when something caught my eye. A giant shadow engulfed the cake shop entrance. It was gone as quickly as it was there, causing me to question if I was seeing things.

Deep in my gut, I knew something was wrong. I turned and ran as fast as my feet would carry me in the opposite direction of my home.

I saw an overturned carriage come into view on my right and heard a growl coming from behind the dress shop. I pressed my back against the shop and took another look at the carriage. The side I could see had a huge dent like something had tried to get in. The door to the carriage was open wide and hanging to the side.

With my back still against the wall, I edged closer to where the wall ended. I peeked around the corner, my heart leaping into my throat at the enormous demon looming over the street. His body was muscular and red, like the colour of blood. His eyes were glowing red, and he had two big, black horns protruding from his head. I had never seen this particular demon in any of the books I'd read or my mother's grimoire, which made me nervous. I'd be going into this fight blind.

I heard a scream and my focus snapped away from the demon to see a girl with her back pressed up against the wall, shaking. Her white shirt was torn and covered in blood. Her long blonde hair was strapped back in a ponytail and swayed in the wind past her hips. She looked familiar but I couldn't place her. The poor girl was horrified, and with a surge of adrenaline and a need to protect her, I sprinted toward them both. I just hoped the Witch Hunters didn't interrupt because then I'd be toast with jam.

As the demon stalked towards the girl, I snuck around the back of him. He was almost upon her, and I was so close to him. I drew my sword from my back when suddenly he stopped and sniffed the air.

Fuck.

He spun his hulking head around and when he saw me, he flung his arm out, hitting me in the stomach. My body and sword flew through the air. I landed with a heavy thud on the ground closer to the overturned carriage while my sword clanged on the ground between us. Pain lanced through my ribs as the breath was knocked from my lungs. I got to my feet, panic rising within me as the demon turned back around and began approaching the girl again.

"Stop!" I managed to choke out while still trying to catch my breath.

The demon turned again and let out a roar, blood and spit flying everywhere. If the Witch Hunters were close by, they'd all be running by now.

"You dare challenge me?" the demon cackled menacingly, his voice reverberated in my ears.

"Just let the girl go and you can take me." I started moving towards him slowly, clutching my ribs as I struggled to suck in air.

I stopped when I heard his loud bellowing laugh. "Or I could take you both."

"You can try," I said back, trying to stand tall and strong.

I was faking a confidence I didn't feel at all. Especially when I realised my hand was empty, my sword still laying on the ground.

When the demon pulled out a curved, behemoth sword from his back, I was eating my words. How I missed seeing that enormous thing I had no idea. I gulped.

"Let's get this over with then." I cursed the wobble in my voice, as a blood chilling grin spread over the demon's hideous face.

"Any final words before I gut you?" the demon sneered.

"It is not I who should be concerned with last words, demon."

He roared with laughter and the girl behind him looked terrified for me.

I couldn't blame her, I was terrified for me.

What was I thinking? This demon was clearly not a lower demon. Which meant he had to be part of Lilith's inner circle. They were far too strong for one mortal witch. I shook the thoughts from my head as the demon slowly and confidently made its way over to me. He was prolonging the moment, instilling fear into his prey.

Demons were sadistic pricks.

I ran for my sword still laying on the ground when the demon raised his behemoth sword over his head and tried to bring it down on me, but I was too quick. I snatched my sword and quickly rolled to the right, dodging his attack. His sword smashed into the stone ground, cracking the walkway, the noise echoed jarringly in my ears. As I skittered backwards, I found myself hoping after all, that the sound would draw the Witch Hunters. If it was a choice between facing them, or facing this demon on my own, I would pick them in a heartbeat. I didn't know how I was going to make it out of this alive.

He lifted his sword and tried a different tactic but reading his stance, I saw it coming. As he swung the sword around, I ducked just in time. I gulped heavily. The bastard had almost cut me in half!

"I can do this all night, little witch. You, however, will tire soon." His voice was deep and frightening.

Dammit, the prick was right. I'd have one chance to take him out, but if I didn't move soon, I'd be too worn out to take it. I summoned fire in my hand and threw a ball towards his face which he annoyingly deflected with his sword. So, I summoned fire again and this time I threw it at his shoulder, anticipating that he'd think I'd go low this time. I was right, he moved his sword down towards his legs to shield them, my fireball striking him in the shoulder. He staggered back several paces, grunting from the pain and seething with frustration.

While he recovered from my blow, I chanced a glance around. The girl wasn't where I'd seen her last, but a flash of blonde from behind a nearby tree told me she'd been smart enough to get out of danger. Good. It meant I could solely focus on getting rid of the demon and didn't have to worry about where she was.

The demon staggered to his feet and lunged for me with a blood curdling roar. I waited until he was just about to bring his sword down on me before sliding between his gigantic legs and slicing my sword across his thigh. He let out another roar and turned around.

My pride at wounding him was stifled when he grabbed me, wrapping his large hand around my neck and pushing me back until my body hit the dress shop wall with a brutal force that knocked the wind out of my lungs. The demon was smiling as my panic rose while he was choking the life out of me. The pain was becoming intense, I felt like I was about to pass out as my eyes started to roll to the back of my head, but I quickly closed them and opened them to try and gain some of my vision back. I focused and clawed at my neck, trying to get a small breath in when suddenly, from the corner of my eye, I saw two figures jump out of the opening of the carriage and head towards us. Everything was starting to blur, the pain overwhelming. I couldn't even focus enough to summon my fire.

The figure's voices around me sounded like they were under-water. I watched one of the blurry figures draw his pistol, cock it and fire directly at the demon. He dropped me to the ground, and I coughed, massaging my now bruised neck. I clutched at my spinning head, sucking in desperate breaths through my battered throat while the demon was distracted. When I finally caught my breath, I staggered to my feet, gripping the wall of the dress shop for support.

The demon roared at the men but stopped mid-roar. He sniffed the air and glanced towards them, smiling.

"Interesting." He made his way to the men.

I leaned against the building and as my vision finally came back to me I noticed one of the men was the Witch Hunter who had saved me the night before. My breath caught in my throat at the realisation He dodged the demon's moves and sliced here and there with his sword in a flurry of steel. He was a glorious fighter, it was mesmerising to watch. The demon somehow didn't seem to be tiring, but the Witch Hunter was and I gasped as the demon sliced a claw across his arm. It was just a small bleeding scratch but it still made him stagger, pain evident in his features.

I ran towards the fight, drew a dagger from my side and stabbed the demon in the back of the leg. The dagger wouldn't come back out so I slowly moved backwards as he roared and ripped it out, black ichor seeping out of the wound. He turned to me and before I could make another move, he plunged the dagger into my stomach. I screamed as white hot pain lanced through the side of my stomach, and I stumbled, my hand clutching just below my ribs. Blood was gushing between my fingers as I fell to the ground on my knees.

The demon was smiling as I knelt there. "Where are those last words now, witchling?"

Blood sprayed across my face, and his head, frozen in that mocking leer, toppled sideways and rolled away on the cobblestones as his body fell with a resounding thump in front of me.

I fell forward onto the ground, gripping my stomach as blood continued to ooze out of my very large wound. Then, as I saw the Witch Hunter running towards me, the edges of my vision blurred and the world went dark.

CHAPTER 7

FENRIS

The demon's head thumped to the ground and rolled away, a trail of stinking ichor in its wake. Another thump had me turning, racing in the direction of the witch. Her body was unmoving on the ground, blood oozing rapidly from a huge gash in her side.

I removed my cloak, throwing it at George as he approached and then I ripped the bottom of my shirt, bunching up the material and pressing it firmly against her wound. As I lifted her into my arms, George placed my cloak over her body, the weight of it keeping the material in place over her wound.

Looking down at her pale face, I noticed her lips first, how they quivered as her eyes flickered. How they were pinkish and plump. I looked back up and shook my head, trying to rid my thoughts and stop my racing heart. I didn't know this girl, and she was a witch. She could very well try and kill me for all I knew.

"A witch saved our lives." Lyra glanced down at the girl in my arms with her mouth open.

The makeshift bandage I had made out of part of my shirt was already soaked in blood and seeping into my cloak. She was losing too much too fast.

"George, grab my satchel from the carriage," I asked as we all raced over.

George rummaged through my satchel and brought out a bandage. I moved the witch around so George could remove the cloak and soaked material and dress the wound. He then placed his hand firmly against the dressing to ensure the pressure would keep the blood from flowing freely.

"We need to do something. We can't just let her die," I said, my tone worried even though I barely knew her. I just knew we had to save her even though it went against everything we were taught to do with her kind.

"The tunnels. We can take her to the apothecary down there," Lyra suggested.

"He will work on anyone, and he won't talk," George added.

"Yes, I think you're both right, it's the safest and quickest option."

"Just keep an eye out. We don't need to run into any more demons," I said and Lyra replied "Or Witch Hunters. Considering you are currently carrying a witch."

Shit. She had a point. The aroma from the witch's blood was already dancing in the air around us. The bitter, earthy scent clung to my nose, my eyes watering from how strong it was. George and Lyra wouldn't be able to smell it. To them, her blood would just smell like normal, coppery blood.

Upon completion of our training, Witch Hunters were given necklaces, among other essential items. These necklaces had runes etched on them that allowed us the ability to smell witch's blood. If another Witch Hunter came close, they'd smell it in an instant.

It wasn't going to be easy, moving her through the streets, considering the closest hidden entry was in an abandoned house closer to the heart of the town. Nobody knew about that entrance but Logan, myself, the princess, George and the king.

We hastily made our way in the direction of the abandoned house. The streets were deserted. I never thought I'd be grateful for a demon attack until now - people hiding in their homes meant less chance of us being discovered transporting an injured witch, and I was too exhausted to have to explain myself.

I peered down at her wound. The bandage was now soaked in blood but her chest was still rising and falling, giving me hope.

"We need to hurry. I don't know how much longer she's got," I said, my heart racing.

We ran as fast as we could the rest of the way. I strained with the weight of the woman in my arms, but we finally made it to the abandoned house without further incidents. We moved to the backyard where George pulled out a key from where it was hidden in a tree. He opened the front door and we all quickly made it inside. George closed the door and locked it behind us.

This house once belonged to the Witch Hunter leader, Daxton before Logan. When he died it was agreed that nobody else would live here. He had the tunnel system connected to his house when he was first promoted to leader for easier access to the church and castle.

The musty smell instantly hit me like it always did. Plants had started growing inside, and there was a hole in the roof where I could see the stars high in the sky. The moon peeked through the cracks, offering its light and casting shadows against the walls. The bookcase to the right was riddled with mould and books were strewn within or on the ground in front of it.

We made our way to the back of the house, where we would find the cellar with the entrance to the tunnels. George lifted up the rug that hid the cellar door and gestured for us to enter once he lifted the hatch. Lyra descended the stairs first, I followed closely behind her, holding the witch tightly to my chest. My muscles were beginning to tire, but we weren't much farther away. George grabbed some flint out of his pocket and a dagger, lighting the torch on the far-right wall. He shut the cellar door, grabbing the torch and moving behind me.

The tunnels were incredibly dark and humid. The torch only illuminated a few feet into the pitch blackness. Thankfully we all knew where we were going. We took several turns, keeping our pace as hurried as we could in the small area we had to walk in.

When we finally arrived at the entrance of the apothecary's dwelling, George hung the torch in an empty sconce since the apothecary kept this part of the tunnel well illuminated. It was an open area, his work table in the middle had tools, bottles, and jars of salves strewn all over. Herbs hung above the table drying. His bed sat in the far-left corner and a second bed for patients in the far-right corner. He was sitting in his chair reading a book, but he got to his feet as we entered.

"What's going on?" he asked, looking towards the girl.

"She's been stabbed in the stomach. Please. Can you help

her?" I asked, my voice frantic.

The apothecary moved towards the girl and checked her over. "Place her on the bed and I'll see what I can do." He gestured to the patient's bed.

I hurried over, laying her limp body down carefully. The witch groaned weakly and I sighed, my body relaxing that she was lucid enough to make a sound at all.

I leant closer as he inspected the wound, but he pressed me backwards with a gentle hand. "I'll need space to work. Best wait in the tunnel hall." He gestured for us to leave.

I hesitated. The thought of leaving the girl, looking so fragile, pale and lifeless on the bed, felt wrong. But when Lyra tapped me on the shoulder, I followed her and George outside. We sat on the dusty ground and waited.

After the first hour, Lyra gave into her exhaustion, her head lolling against my shoulder and her breaths becoming deep and even. George was still on full alert the entire time.

My feelings were conflicted with everything going on. I had just saved this witch for the second time, a being I vowed to eradicate when I became a Witch Hunter. They were supposed to be evil but there didn't seem to be anything evil about her. Why did she save us from that demon? What could she possibly gain from risking her own life for ours, people who hate her kind? The way she moved and the way she fought was admirable, she was definitely trained in combat.

What was taking the apothecary so long? I found myself hoping she would be okay, an ache in my chest forming as we continued to wait. She had lost so much blood, how could she possibly survive? Would she survive? I was so worried about her and I still didn't understand why I cared so much whether a witch would live or die. But then I remembered how her lips looked. The plump pink of them and how they moved with her breaths, it made me breathe harder.

"She's going to be alright." The apothecary interrupted my thoughts. "You can come in and see her now." He wiped his hands with a cloth.

George gently nudged Lyra awake. She stirred before grog-gily getting to her feet.

We made our way back inside and I went to sit next to her as Lyra and George stood behind me. I wondered what she was dreaming about, or if she was dreaming at all. I sighed and Lyra placed her hand on my shoulder.

"What are we going to do with her?" I asked, looking up at Lyra.

It went against everything I was taught, but I found myself hoping the Princess would pardon her. What kind of Witch Hunter hopes for a witch to be let loose? But then I gazed down again and saw how beautiful she was. She was fierce and fiery and something about her called to me, made me want to know more about her.

George finally spoke and the sound of his voice made me jump. "We need to leave before she wakes up." George placed his hand on Lyra's shoulder. "We should get you back to the castle, back to safety, Princess. It's getting late."

"She saved my life, George. I'd like to thank her," Lyra responded firmly.

"Doesn't mean she won't take it away just as easily," he said.

"Where is this coming from? You were fine to let her fight for us, to save us. You were fine to help us bring her here and now all of a sudden you want to just leave her." My voice rose and the apothecary glanced up, putting his finger over his mouth.

"Fen is right. We can't just leave her. We should escort her home at the very least," Lyra argued.

"I disagree. My main concern is and always will be Princess Lyra's safety. She was useful in the fight and we brought her here out of respect for helping us but we don't owe her any more of our time. I think the night has gone on long enough and we should go." George seemed impatient.

"Are you questioning the decision of the Princess?" I asked him, using Lyra's title with a hint of challenge in my tone.

"You're overstepping your station, Witch Hunter," George sneered, taking a threatening step toward me.

It was very unusual to see him like this, but I suppose I had never witnessed him having to protect Lyra since she's mostly been locked up in the castle.

"Okay. I have an idea," Lyra said, and we both looked towards her. "Fen will escort this girl home. George and I will make our way through the tunnels and back into the castle. Everyone is happy," she finished.

George hmphed but nodded and I let out a huge breath. I was relieved to know I wouldn't have to leave the witch by herself. I was also relieved I didn't have to go head to head with George.

Lyra grabbed my hand. "Will you tell her I said thank you?"

"Of course I will."

A whimper erupted from the bed, and we all turned. My heart leapt into my chest. The girl, the witch, was sitting up, her piercing green eyes fixed on me.

CHAPTER 8

MARELLA

M y head was throbbing, my magic barely more than a glowing ember inside me. I couldn't have opened my eyes if I wanted to, but nearby voices burbled. If I wanted to know where I was, I was going to have to eavesdrop. Maybe then I could understand what was going on. My mind was foggy and my memory of what happened to me was blurry.

"Fen will escort this girl home. George and I will make our way through the tunnels and back into the castle. Everyone is happy," a smooth, female voice said.

The events of the night came back to me in a rush. The higher demon. The pain of my own dagger as it pierced my side. The Witch Hunter, almost fighting alongside me. And there had been a girl. Maybe it was this girl. I opened my eyes and sat up on whatever uncomfortable bed I was lying on. Three sets of eyes snapped to me. One pair wide, hazel, below raised blonde brows belonging to the girl from the street. A dark pair set in a furrowed brow of a very large, scowling man. And one pair intensely blue, filled with some emotion I couldn't decipher. Those ones belonged to the Witch Hunter. The one who had saved my life twice now.

"Where am I?" My voice was shaky.

"You are in the underground tunnels. My name is Lyra, and this is Fenris and George," the girl I had protected said as she pointed towards the two men.

My eyes widened. "You're Princess Lyra! I knew you looked familiar, I just couldn't place you. I rarely venture into town." I fiddled with my fingers.

I was in the presence of royalty, something I never thought would ever happen to me. She was stunning with her long blonde hair and the way she held herself with such confidence. I was jealous of that confidence. It was something I had always lacked with how we had to hide ourselves away all the time for fear of being caught. But now that she had caught me, would she get rid of me?

"I am. I swear I won't turn you in." Princess Lyra's tone was gentle. She must have seen the worry on my face.

"Why wouldn't you?" I asked carefully.

"Why would I turn someone in that saved my life and the lives of my friends?"

"But... I'm a witch." I had no idea why I was trying to give her reasons to lock me away.

"A brave witch." She smiled softly. "What is your name?"

"Marella. You can call me Ella, if it pleases you, Your Highness." I had never met royalty before so I was unsure what I was supposed to say in her presence. I had read books before so copied what I had learned from them.

She moved carefully towards me but I looked over at the two men, remembering that the one she named Fenris was the one who saved me from Andras. I was shocked to finally learn his name. Fenris. I liked that name.

I slid off the bed, wincing in pain, my hand moving to my bandaged side. Fenris moved towards me, concern lacing his features.

"You saved me," I said.

"You helped take down that demon, so I'd say you saved yourself as much as I saved you," he answered.

I, of course, wasn't referring to the fight with the demon but he gave me a pleading look, so I didn't speak further on our first encounter.

A man appeared, wearing the unmistakable brown cloak and gold brooch of an apothecary. His eyebrows went up when he saw me.

"Ah. You're awake. Excellent. Take a teaspoon of this mixture in the morning and before bed for the next three days for any pain." The man grabbed a vial of blue liquid from a shelf and handed it to me. I knew it was a pain tonic because Hulda made some for when she was too exhausted to use her healing magic.

"Thank you for looking after me," I said.

"You're welcome, ma'am. Now, you are standing but you seem to be swaying somewhat. Are you alright or do you need to sit down for a little longer?" He placed his hand on my forearm which helped keep me steady.

"I'll be fine."

"Your wound is extreme, you're lucky you did not die. A moment longer and you very well may have," the apothecary tsked. "Be careful not to move or stretch too much over the next couple of days or you'll reopen the wound."

I didn't plan on having the wound for that long. The second I was home I would ask Hulda to heal it for me. So, I just nodded at him in agreement.

"Now, I would thank you all to leave so I can get some reading done before bed." He made a shooing gesture towards us.

Princess Lyra handed the apothecary a pouch. "For your troubles."

"Thank you, Princess." He took the pouch and bowed.

"Thank you again," I said to him, and we all moved out into the hall of the tunnel.

After exiting the apothecary's space, I glanced to the right and the left of the tunnels. All I could make out was a long hallway made entirely of stone. It was dark with only the torch Fenris now held lighting the area. He grabbed an unlit torch from the wall, used his to light it and handed it to George. The tunnel was vast and unfamiliar, but somehow I felt safe around these people. I shouldn't feel safe around them, not at all. One of them was a Witch Hunter, sworn to kill my kind. One was the Princess, whose father funded these Witch Hunters. The other was a Royal Guard, it seemed as though he was Princess Lyra's personal guard.

I took a breath in and out and told myself, if they wanted to kill me, they'd had more than enough opportunity while I was unconscious.

"Fenris can escort you home now that you're awake. It's late and I would hate for something to happen to you," Lyra said, she had a very soothing voice. She had this presence about her that made me want to be her friend. Could a witch be friends with a Princess? I brushed the thought aside, it was a fool's hope, and a dangerous one.

"We must get back to the castle now," George said.

"Stay safe, Ella." Princess Lyra took my hand, her warmth seeping into my cool palms. She squeezed my hand reassuringly, comforting me.

A Witch Hunter, Princess and Royal Guard had saved my life. My eyes darted between the three of them, causing my vision to blur momentarily. I stumbled, but Fenris managed to hold me close to him. His hands were warm against my arm, his touch gentle.

"Thank you, Princess. I appreciate your discretion and for paying the apothecary. You didn't have to do that." I hope I sounded calm, when everything inside of me was churning.

"Nonsense, it's the least I could do. I wish there was more I could do for you for saving my life." Princess Lyra dropped her gaze, her fingers twisted around themselves.

She wasn't like most Royals I had heard of. That surprised me. I still couldn't get over how kind she was. It was throughout our entire history that the Royals were not to be trusted, yet, Princess Lyra was nothing like that. She was gentle, confident and kind. She wasn't going to turn me in. I felt so grateful towards her.

"Shall we head out... Ella?" Fenris asked.

"I'm ready whenever you are." I felt exhausted and my side was starting to hurt.

"You should seek Fenris out, if you ever need us," the Princess said with a warm smile.

"Thank you." I smiled back, trying to be polite and hiding the nervous lilt in my voice.

George put his hand on Princess Lyra's back and led her away, the light from their torch fading with them.

I looked back at Fenris. "Lead the way."

"Right. Okay. This way." He cleared his throat, sounding somewhat nervous, which struck me as odd.

I placed my hand over his arm. "Do you want to see something?" My breath caught as he gazed at me with those blue eyes. His cheeks turned pink as he looked away and I moved back.

I summoned a ball of fire that hovered in the air and would trail us until I extinguished it. Fenris stared at it in awe and I saw a lick of fear cross his features, causing me to flinch, but I tried not to react further. He hung up the torch he had since we no longer needed it to illuminate our way out. My firelight bounced softly off the walls of the tunnel.

Fenris took the lead as we started walking. I'd never seen a Witch Hunter act the way he did. He seemed... different. I watched him as he walked, his focus was like none I had ever seen. Whenever I had run-ins with Andras he was always cruel and calculated. He wanted to kill me and he always had a look of disgust on his face, like the very sight of me made him sick to his stomach. Fenris wasn't like that at all. He seemed almost happy to be in my presence.

"Why did you save me?" I asked suddenly, curiosity getting the better of me.

"Why do you want to know?"

"I'm intrigued." I shrugged my shoulders.

He stopped for a moment and turned to look at me. "We aren't all the same, Witch Hunters, I mean. I don't hate your kind. I just... I don't know." He furrowed his brows, thinking. "You were trying to save the Princess. That shows me that you're not evil. That you aren't at all what we've been taught. It confuses me a little, if I'm being honest."

His response shocked me into silence.

He began walking again and I followed, watching the way he moved, the way he carried himself. What was he thinking right now? Does he really mean it when he says he doesn't hate my kind? It was scary, trying to learn to trust when you had never been close to someone before. Hulda was always there for me, it was true, but she was my mother figure at this point. I wanted to believe I could have this. Have friends that knew who I was and didn't shy away from it. But could I? Could they be trusted? I was finding it hard to believe that a Witch Hunter harboured no hate for witches, but yet here Fenris was, proving that he didn't.

"So, where do these tunnels lead to anyway? They seem so long." Greta had already told me but I wanted to see what he would tell me, if he felt he could trust me enough.

He hesitated a moment. "They lead to the castle and the church."

"I'm surprised you told me that," I confided.

"Well, technically you can't enter the castle or church anyway. Being a Witch and all," he said matter-of-factly.

"What would happen if I did?"

"Let's just say you don't want to test it and find out."

"Okay then," I said with a surprised nod, quite sure he was telling the truth and it was better if I didn't know after all.

The tunnel abruptly ended, but I could see a small set of stairs and a trap door. We climbed the stairs and the door creaked loudly as Fenris pushed it open. Light bathed the tunnel, so I extinguished my flame as we made our way out.

I stepped into a house that had clearly not been lived in for a long time. The floors were falling apart and the furniture was dirty with all sorts of plants running over them. The air was pungent with the smell of mould, it was musty and damp and whenever I'd breath in, it would tickle my nostrils. There was a furry growth on all the furniture, rotting it. It made my skin crawl.

"What is this place?" I asked, hiding the disgust on my face as I stepped out of the tunnel entrance. I watched as Fenris closed the trap door and moved a rug over it.

"This used to be the house of a Witch Hunter leader. As you can see, nobody has lived here since."

"You don't say!" I rolled my eyes. He ignored my sarcasm.

"So why is it left unattended? Aren't you worried people will try to infiltrate the castle?" I furrowed my eyebrows.

"Nobody knows the entrance exists, it would be highly unlikely for someone to stumble upon it and if they did they'd be met with a sword to the stomach by one of the several guards or Witch Hunters, depending on which way they went," he answered. I chose not to press, the message was read loud and clear.

"Where to now then?" I changed the subject.

"We will have to keep to the shadows and try to remain on the back streets. I can't have anyone notice me." Fenris moved towards the front door.

"You mean you don't want anyone to notice you with a witch. You can just say that."

"That's not what I meant. I don't want either of us to get hurt. Which we will be if we're caught."

"Because I'm a witch and your people hate us for no reason?" My voice rose in anger. I was so sick of having to live like this.

He sighed and gazed up at me. "Ella, I'm sorry for everything you've been through, for how you've had to live. I don't hate you, if that's any consolation. But the reality is, if another

Witch Hunter found us, it would be both of us on the chopping block. You know that." He appealed to the rational part of my brain.

My anger dissipated because as much as it annoyed me, he was right. He really meant every word he said and there was honour in that.

"Okay. I apologise for snapping at you. It takes a long time to unlearn a way of living, I guess." I took a deep breath in and out, releasing the rest of that anger. "I live within the Fraying Forests. How do we get there from here?" I asked.

I hated that I had to rely on someone to get me home. I never ventured into the heart of the town often so I had no idea where we actually were. I only knew where the tavern was and Walter's house because we went there so often. I knew that our cottage was south of Hayselwood but I wasn't sure where we currently were. But once we were in the Fraying Forests I'd have to ditch him. I couldn't have him finding out where I lived and risking Hulda's life as well as my own.

"Follow me." He led me out the back door and we moved quietly and carefully. I followed closely behind. "We don't have to go too far. If we keep following the backs of these houses we'll come to the Fraying Forests. We just need to be careful that nobody in the houses sees us and alerts Witch Hunters."

"But you are a Witch Hunter. Won't they just think you're doing the rounds?" I questioned.

"If I was alone I'd get away with that. With you, not so much." He smirked playfully.

"Stick to the shadows. Got it."

We started manoeuvring through bushes and avoiding any light that trickled along the ground from the stars and moon.

Now that it was getting later into the night, the cold air

brushed against my face and I knew my nose was turning red. Goosebumps crawled up my arms. The wound on my stomach was beginning to throb lightly with the cold. I shivered while clutching the wall of a house. I could see the mist coming out of Fenris' mouth as he breathed but he didn't seem bothered by the cold.

He moved from one area to another and I followed close behind. We finally made it to the edge of the woods and Fenris took my hand, leading me to a tree to hide behind so we were out of view.

"Where to now?" Fenris asked.

"I can see myself home from here. Thank you," I replied. No way was I leading a Witch Hunter to my home.

"I don't know if that's a good idea. You were stabbed in the stomach not that long ago and now you want to venture into the forests by yourself?" He crossed his arms.

"You forget, I'm a Witch. My fire will protect me against my enemies."

"That doesn't change the fact you are still hurt. You're not invincible just because you're a witch. I think tonight proves that," he argued.

"I know that. I just... I don't feel comfortable sharing the location of my home with someone I just met... especially not a Witch Hunter. Forget it."

Fenris uncrossed his arms and slung them to his side. "Okay, fine. But please be careful. Get home as quickly as possible."

"Before you go I just wanted to thank you... for everything. You didn't have to save me twice, but you did." I smiled, looking up into his eyes. "I'm curious though, why are you a Witch Hunter? You just don't seem to enjoy your job."

"It's all I've ever known and trained for. I grew up in the

castle and it was either Witch Hunter or Royal Guard. Being a Witch Hunter appealed to me more."

"Have you killed witches before?" I hugged my arms close, rubbing them to warm myself.

He hesitated and gazed down at the ground. "No, I haven't killed a witch before. But I have been present when witches have been killed."

"Oh. That's.... interesting. Why have you been around but not actually killed a witch yourself?" The subject made my stomach churn but I had to know.

"I never felt the need. All the witches I've met have seemed so... normal. There was a coven recently that... I think it'll stay with me forever." He appeared as though he was blinking back tears. Whatever happened must have affected him greatly.

"Do you want to talk about it?" I asked gently.

He cleared his throat. "Maybe another time. You have to get home. Do you have a coven or anyone at home waiting for you?"

"It's just myself and Hulda." I scolded myself for telling him about who I was living with. I may have trusted him, but I should have been more careful sharing information that could potentially be used against me.

"I feel like we have it all wrong about witches. You seem just like us and besides, you risked your life to save us, to save the Princess, knowing she could have you killed. You almost did lose your life tonight."

That surprised me. "Well. Thank you for your words. For tonight, as well. Also, the other night. You saved my life twice now but who's counting."

"Don't mention it," he replied.

I held out my hand and as he shook it, he winced in pain. I

saw the bandage wrapped around his hand and remembered his fight with Andras. How he was hit with Andras' branding iron.

"Well, you were more than happy to injure yourself for my safety... I can heal that for you, if you like." I went to grab his hand, but just as we touched he pulled back so fast I thought his hand was going to snap off.

His face said it all. His mouth slightly opened and his eyebrows raised, eyes widened. He gulped as he held his hand against his chest.

"Yeah. You don't hate witches, right? I should have known better. You're a liar and you're all the same. Ugh." I walked off and although I heard him call out my name, I ignored him and headed for home.

CHAPTER 9

FENRIS

I was in my room getting ready for the day when my bedroom door burst open. I must have forgotten to lock it last night. It came as no surprise to see a scowling Logan enter my room.

"Princess Lyra said you were attacked by a higher demon last night! Care to explain?" Anger laced his tone.

We never really kept secrets from each other. Technically, something like this, I should have gone straight to him and told him.

"Yes. Look, Logan, I'm sorry I didn't say anything. I didn't want to worry you. We took care of it, and nobody got hurt." *Except for Ella who was thankfully healed in time*, a snarky voice inside my head said.

"Why was the Princess even outside the castle walls at

night?" Logan demanded.

"I can't say. She has sworn me to secrecy. You know I would tell you if I could, Logan but she ordered me not to tell a soul."

"It better have been for a damn good reason if you were willing to let her risk her life." He paced the room for a moment then turned back to me. "We had several demons attack the town last night and we could have really used your help. The fact you were off somewhere doing who knows what really pisses me off, Fenris."

"I'm sorry, Logan. I know," I pleaded with him again.

He cut me off before I could say more. "I want a full report on my desk by the end of the day." He turned and stormed out, slamming the door behind him.

I sighed and rubbed my hands over my stubble. Logan was angry, rightfully so, but there was nothing I could do to fix that right now. I had bigger problems.

Thinking over the past night's events, I recalled my departure from Ella. She was also mad at me. I was annoyed with myself for making her think I feared or even hated her kind. I wasn't sure what to think if I was being honest with myself. All I had ever been taught was that witches were evil and we had to rid the world of them or they'd kill us first. How was I supposed to throw all of that out the window when it was all I'd ever known? I wanted to trust Ella and I wanted to believe in her, but what if I was wrong? What if all we had been taught was true after all?

I shook my head from my thoughts because the truth was, I flinched because her touch was electrifying, and it scared me. She was a witch, and I was a Witch Hunter. I was afraid of what it meant.

I was thankful that Lyra and George at least didn't tell Logan about her. I knew what Logan was like and he wouldn't take kindly to us harbouring a witch, saving her even. He wouldn't stand for it and I was fearful of what he might do. Not just to Ella, but to me. I was his best friend but would that friendship hold strong if he knew what I had done? It made me wonder why Lyra told Logan of our encounter in the first place. I supposed it was better for her to say something than me. It was hard to lie to Logan when I'd known him my whole life.

I sighed and walked out the door, heading to the front of the castle where I knew I'd find Lyra.

She was sitting in her usual seat that was placed in front of a window, overlooking the castle grounds and giving her a view of every single coming and going. Lyra always said she liked knowing before anyone else in the castle who was approaching. I always told her she was being nosey.

She held a thick book in her hands and was pondering the pages with such focus. I walked towards her, and she looked up.

"Fen, how are you?" she asked, closing her book.

"Why would you tell Logan about last night, Lyra? You know he's not going to let it go now," I demanded, more forcefully than I had intended.

"It was a high demon, Fen. I couldn't not tell the leader of the Witch Hunters. Plus, Logan has a way of getting things out of me and he told me there were several reports of a commotion near the castle gates. I had to tell him." She got to her feet and squeezed my arm. "I'm sorry, Fen. I stand by telling him. It was a high demon for goodness sake!"

Although I was frustrated at the current circumstances, I knew she was right. Logan, as the leader of the Witch Hunters, had a right to know.

I sighed in resignation. "You're right. Thank you for not telling him about Ella." I sat beside her, our seats next to each other.

"Oh, I wouldn't dream of it. That girl helped save my life. Speaking of her, did she get home safe?" she enquired gently, concern evident in her tone.

"I got her as close to home as she'd let me... but we didn't part on good terms," I confessed.

Lyra narrowed her brows. "What did you do?"

"Why do you assume it was me?"

"You forget I grew up with you." She let out a laugh.

"She tried to use her magic to heal me and I *may* have flinched away. She took it the wrong way and stormed off."

"Oh Fen, you silly goose! What other way is she supposed to take that? You're a Witch Hunter for goodness sake. Of course she took it that way. What were you thinking?" Lyra shook her head and clipped me over the head.

"Um...ouch." I rubbed the tender spot.

Lyra laughed and crossed her arms. "You deserve more than that. Be more careful next time."

George walked into the room and bowed towards Lyra, interrupting our conversation. "Your father requests your presence, Princess. He also wants Fenris there too."

"We will talk more about this later, Fen," Lyra whispered, glaring at me.

We both got to our feet and walked behind George, my nerves evident as I fumbled around with my hands and kept brushing my hair out of my face. The King was going to be angrier than Logan was and I was not looking forward to the verbal lashing I was about to receive.

George opened the big brass doors leading into the bigger

meeting room within the castle. There were four long, open arched windows to the right that let in a significant amount of light, draping over the table in the middle of the room. The room was mostly empty except for the table, twelve chairs around it and a desk to the left with scrolls and paper stuffed into the drawers. The King was sitting in the tallest of the seats, rubies glinting around the top, scattering red light around the room. He was reading some papers but looked up as we entered.

"King Aldric. I hope we didn't keep you waiting too long," I said as I bowed my head respectfully. He gestured for Lyra and I to take a seat.

"You can leave George. I've already dealt with you." King Aldric waved him off. George bowed at the waist, then left the room, shutting the doors behind him with a resounding boom, sealing us inside to our fate.

"What were you both thinking last night?" King Aldric rose to his feet as anger passed over his features, not wasting any time in berating us.

"Lyra, you know you're not allowed out of this castle at night. Fenris, you should know better than to escort the Princess on one of her misguided adventures. You fight these things every damned night so you know the dangers they pose. You both could have been killed," he yelled, his voice echoing around the room in his anger. I thought how pointless it was telling George to leave since he would have been able to hear it all anyway while he stood behind those doors.

"Father, I'm sorry. Fenris didn't want to go. He tried to talk me out of it but I wouldn't let it go," Lyra appealed to the King, her father.

"I'm sorry, Your Majesty. I should have stopped her and told you immediately," I interrupted.

Lyra shot me a look that told me she would handle it, but I wasn't going to sit here and allow her to take all of the blame. It was my fault too for even allowing it to happen.

"Why did you need to leave these walls so badly that you risked your life and those of your companions? Your friends?" King Aldric accused Lyra.

"I just wanted to see how things were doing outside of the castle, that's all. I lost track of time." She lied so easily.

My jaw dropped open. Why was Lyra lying to her father? Keeping what we'd learned from her spies from the King would never end well. I snapped my mouth closed when she glared at me, staring daggers into my soul. I glared right back at her. We both snapped our heads up as King Aldric started talking.

"Fenris, you've been here since you were a young child. I care for you as if you were my own son. I don't want to see you hurt just as much as I don't want to see Lyra hurt. You both need to be more careful. I'll be placing you under extra guard, Lyra and you are no longer to leave the castle unless I approve of it first. Is that clear?" King Aldric's tone left no room for argument from me, but Lyra was never going to take that for an answer. She always had to fight instead of obey.

"Father, that's insanity. You can't just dictate my comings and goings!" she argued.

"As your father... and your King, I most certainly can. You're lucky I didn't dismiss George permanently for letting you galavant around. It's only because he has been with you, protecting you since birth that I'm allowing him to stay." He looked at me. "I want you to inform Logan of all your comings and goings as well, Fenris. I won't have either of you getting hurt or, perish the thought, killed." He sat back down in his seat.

95

I clenched my fists under the table, my jaw twitching with annoyance. However, I could understand his position, so I replied, "Of course, Your Majesty."

Lyra scoffed and slouched in her chair.

"George, please come in," King Aldric shouted towards the door.

They opened wide and George walked over to the King.

"Please escort Princess Lyra to her room and make sure she has three guards with her at all times. Do not let her out of your sight or let her leave this castle again. If you do so you will be relieved of your duties, am I understood?"

"Yes, Your Majesty," George bowed and headed towards Lyra.

She got to her feet, rolled her eyes, and left with him. I got out of the chair and started heading to the door but turned as the King spoke.

"Sometimes I wish I never allowed you to become a Witch Hunter. I worry about you every day." He sighed and gestured for me to leave.

I bowed and walked out the doors, almost colliding with Logan.

"Look, I'm still furious with you and we will deal with that later. But I need you to come with me to a meeting tomorrow night. You're the only person I trust." He was anxious, I could tell by the tone of his voice.

"What's going on? What's the meeting for?" I asked, moving him to the side so we were out of the way of the doors.

"It's one of our newer, younger scholars. Greta. She said it's important we speak in private. Finish your report on that demon from last night then spend the remainder of the day resting and I'll meet you at the church tomorrow night before the sun goes down."

"I'll be there," I answered.

"Good man," Logan nodded and walked away. I headed to my room to complete the report.

I was confused about why he had been in such a hurry to inform me of the meeting. He could have found me in my quarters later in the day. It worried me how anxious he seemed. Logan rarely felt those kinds of emotions. He was always headstrong. Which begged the question, what was going on?

CHAPTER 10

MARELLA

I spent the majority of the day sleeping after Hulda had fully healed me. When I woke up it was to the smell of breakfast, wafting into my room. I made my way out to the kitchen and found Hulda hard at work like she always was. I took a seat and placed my head in my hands.

"I am so exhausted," I mumbled.

"Well, you almost died last night. Would have, in fact, if it hadn't been for that human apothecary," she said over the steaming stove.

My stomach churned, bile rising up my throat at the memory of the vision I had regarding my death. I had known it wasn't going to be from that higher demon stabbing me, I knew I'd live beyond that. But the fear took over knowing my death would come soon and I had no idea when exactly it would happen.

Just being in the cottage made my heart race. What if she was on her way at this very moment?

"I'm thankful he patched me up," I forced myself to say as I swallowed my fear.

"You are looking a lot better now though." She looked me up and down and gave a nod of approval.

"Thank you, for healing what he couldn't last night. I do wish this exhaustion would go away though," I groaned.

"You'll be feeling like that for a while unfortunately. Healing doesn't just take a lot from me; it can take a lot from the injured as well," she explained.

I had seen it in some of her more injured patients before, so I wasn't surprised I felt like this. I just hadn't known how bone deep the exhaustion would go.

"Hulda, do you know much about Scree Demons?" I tried not to sound suspicious but my voice failed me.

She was immediately wary, and I scolded myself for broaching the subject so randomly.

"Just that they can predict the future but you already know that. Why?" She squinted her eyes.

"I'm just trying to learn more, that's all. Do their visions always come true?" I asked as Hulda put a bowl of soup in front of me with bread on the side.

She took a seat opposite me. "I've never encountered one before or know much about their visions so I can't answer that sorry. Why, Ella? Did something happen?"

"Nothing happened, don't worry about it. I was just wondering." I started slurping up my soup to cover my nerves.

I knew she could see right through me but she didn't press me any further. We sat and ate our soup, chatting about trivial things like whose turn it was to cut the firewood for the next couple of nights. It was mine.

"Are you doing anything tonight?" Hulda asked.

"I think I'm going to call in and go back to bed. I have a meeting with Greta tomorrow night, so I want to be as rested as I can," I answered as I finished the last of my bread and soup and got to my feet.

"Good idea. A nice, long rest should fix the exhaustion you're feeling. I'm glad you've made a friend with Greta. Just be careful."

"Aren't I always careful?" I gave her a smile.

She scoffed. "Not nearly as much as I'd like you to be."

I rolled my eyes. "I love you, Hulda, but you worry too much."

"It's my job to worry about you."

I got to my feet and hugged her around the shoulders before heading back to my room.

***

I sucked in a deep breath and released it as I entered the tavern. Scanning the room, I could see the serving girls refilling pitchers of ale or chatting away to some rowdy men, patrons laughing and the chatter filling the room.

Looking over towards where we said we'd meet I could see our table was empty. I grabbed a drink and headed down, hoping Greta would arrive soon and it would put my mind at ease. I hadn't been able to clear my mind of worry for her, that she'd be hurt. If anything had happened to her, I would make it my mission to take down Andras and the Witch Hunters once and for all.

But then there was Fenris. After everything he had done for me, saving me not once, but twice, could I really bring him down if needed? There was something different about him. He didn't seem to fit as a Witch Hunter, I felt like it wasn't his true calling.

I was so consumed with my thoughts that I didn't even realise Greta had shown up until she was sliding into her seat and placing a drink in front of me.

"You made it," I said to her, relief flooding me knowing she was safe. I moved my empty cup of ale out of the way and grasped the new one she had given me.

"It was hard getting away from Andras at first, but he ended up preoccupied with some other Witch Hunters. I took that as my cue to slip out," she said, her breath heavy as though she had run here.

"You won't get caught or in trouble from Andras, will you?" I asked, taking a sip of my ale.

"I left Andras a note saying I needed a breather for the night. I didn't say where I was going, so I'm hoping he doesn't come looking for me. I doubt he will though, he doesn't seem to care much for me." She peered down at her drink.

"Don't take it personally, he doesn't care for anyone. He's an arse," I added. "Has he tried anything since the other night?"

"Surprisingly, no. He seems preoccupied with something else."

That was interesting. I wondered what it was he was up to. Something despicable, no doubt. Probably out torturing witches for the fun of it. I really needed to get rid of the slippery prick.

"So did you speak to Logan or anyone?" I pressed.

She glanced towards the door then back at me. "Actually. Logan will be here soon."

"Wait... what?" I raised my eyebrows and widened my eyes. I knew Logan didn't know I was a witch but being that close to him for a long time could mean he had more of a chance of sniffing me out. I was also fearful that Fenris may have told him. I assumed if that was the case they would have sought me out and killed me by now, but that doubt was always in the back of my mind.

"I'm sorry to ambush you like this, but I got scared when I went to him. I told him I needed a private meeting with him and that I'd like a friend with me for support. He agreed to meet here." She brushed her hair out of her face and drank a mouthful of her ale.

"I wish you would have told me first, gotten word to me somehow. What if he finds out what I am?" My heart was thundering.

"Just don't bleed and you'll be fine. That's how the Witch Hunters can tell who is a witch. They can smell it in your blood," Greta said.

Well, that was new information. Thank god I didn't have my monthlies.

"How can they smell our blood? Only us witches are meant to be able to smell it."

Greta must have noted my surprise, as she softened a fraction in understanding of how little I knew about their world.

"Their runes can uncover a lot. I'll teach you about them sometime," she offered.

"Yeah, that would be good. Thank you." I glanced around, distracted.

I finished my ale and went to grab two more. What was going to happen in this meeting? Would Logan take it all seriously or was he just like Andras? What if he found out what I was even if I didn't bleed? As the leader of the Witch Hunters, maybe he would know. Maybe he could help get rid of Andras or maybe he would throw us both to the dogs. I guess we'd find out soon enough.

I turned from the bar and saw Logan approaching Greta. I didn't even see him come in. I ordered another drink, picking them all up when they were done. I carefully manoeuvred my way through the newly developed crowd to get to the table.

"It's you. What are you doing here?" Logan asked.

"You remember Ella, who saved me from those demon worshippers in the Fraying Forest the other night." Greta's tone was pointed.

"This is Witch Hunter business and she's not a Witch Hunter or a scholar." Logan crossed his arms then turned to me. "We are grateful for what you did, but this is inappropriate."

"I didn't see any Witch Hunters around when I saved Greta. I find it inappropriate that one of your scholars was left unattended," I shot back. "As her friend, Greta's safety is my business now too."

Logan's mouth had fallen open but I ignored him.

I handed Greta her drink and she gave me a thankful smile.

"I'd say it's nice to see you again but this interaction so far has been quite rude given I saved one of your scholars from a bunch of demon worshippers," I went on.

Logan paled as I sat down next to Greta. He opened his mouth to say something, but then snapped it shut, glaring daggers at me. My eyes were suddenly drawn to the door and my breath caught in my throat as I saw Fenris walking in, his presence captivating me as his broad shoulders and tall frame walked through the door. My nerves shuddered through my body as our eyes met for a split second. He stumbled, but quickly righted himself and strode towards the table, taking the seat next to Logan, his expression giving nothing away. I stifled a giggle.

"Fine, you can stay," Logan's voice tore my gaze from Fenris. "This is Fenris by the way. I asked him to join us today because he's my most trusted Witch Hunter," Logan said, patting him on the back. "Fenris, this is Ella. She saved Greta the other day in the woods against several demon worshippers."

Fenris' expression was blank for a moment before he remembered that he wasn't supposed to know me. "Nice to meet you, thank you for helping Greta. Ella was it?" He thrust out a hand for me to shake, pretending to introduce himself. I took it gently, his grip firm and warm.

I sighed with relief that he didn't bring up that we already knew each other. He was pretending not to know me. Good. I didn't want there to be any mishaps and Logan finding out who I was would not be a good time.

"I'm just glad I was there to help," I answered, releasing his hand.

"What brings us here tonight, Greta? And why in the tavern, instead of at the church?" Logan asked as his eyes darted to me for a moment before looking back at Greta.

It was clear he wasn't happy an outsider was present for the meeting. I got the feeling he didn't like me for some reason, which was fine by me. I didn't like him either.

"Well... it's about Andras. He... well... I'm sorry." She stumbled over her words, fiddling with her hands on the table.

"It's okay, Greta." Logan placed his hand over hers in a comforting gesture. "You can confide in us. We are here to help."

A blush creeped over Greta's cheeks, her fingers twitching under his touch and she refused to meet his eye.

"It is my belief that Andras killed Bianca and that witch,"

Greta blurted out and sounded on the verge of tears.

I could tell how frightened she was, so I draped my arm around her for comfort. Fenris and Logan both wore the same shocked expression on their faces as Greta went into detail just as she did with me the other night. Once she was done, she gazed down at the table and sighed.

"Greta, you're safe. I promise you that. We won't let anything happen to you," Logan assured.

"You both don't seem too shocked by this revelation." I crossed my arms.

Fenris looked at Logan then back to me. "Andras has always been a bit of a mystery. He's worked with us for a long time but we don't really know a lot about him. At least, I don't." He looked back to Logan, but he didn't add to what Fenris had said.

That had me seeing red. "So you don't even know the people you have working for you? The people who are patrolling the towns as if they own the place?"

"Hang on just a minute, Ella. We don't have any control over who works for us. King Aldric employs all Witch Hunters and he was the one who appointed Andras." Logan narrowed his eyes on me.

"Well, he did a lousy job then," I scowled, letting my anger get the better of me.

Fenris' eyes widened. "Be careful what you say, Ella. Words against the King could be considered treason," he whispered.

Logan glared at me, his mouth open slightly and his brows furrowed. "What is wrong with you?"

"Nothing is wrong with me, you arse! What is wrong with you?" I got to my feet but Greta grabbed my arm gently and pulled me back down.

"Can we stop this please and get back to the matter at hand." Fenris raised his voice.

"What happens now then?" My voice shook.

"We will assign Greta to someone else for now and thoroughly investigate Andras. Maybe have one of our more stealthier Witch Hunters follow his movements."

"Andras needs to be taken down," I said, annoyance in my tone.

"Ella, you're talking about removing a Witch Hunter with no proof of the allegations. That's not something we can just do. We have protocols in place that need to be followed. Please know that we won't let him get away with it," Fenris lectured me, his mouth stern, but his eyes earnest.

He went to grab my hand but I pulled away just as he touched me. I felt something, I wasn't sure what, but it was something, a tingle or a surge between us.

"I will assign you to me for now. That way I can keep a close eye on you and Andras won't be able to try anything." Logan offered a look of apology for all she'd been through.

"Thank you, Logan. The care you're taking means a lot to me," Greta smiled.

"I will always take care of everyone as best I can. You are all my responsibility and I take pride in my work. For now, I'll take you back to the church and to your room, so I know you're safe. I will then meet you in the morning to start our day."

Greta deflated slightly at his comment about taking care of everyone, but hid it just as quickly.

"What about Andras? He's going to be suspicious that I'm suddenly taken from him," Greta asked, her voice choppy.

"Let me deal with Andras. You don't have to worry or be afraid of him anymore," Logan turned from Greta to me. "Do these plans meet your approval?" he asked me sarcastically.

I scoffed. "You keep Greta safe, and get rid of the scum in your ranks, and then I'll be satisfied. Or I'll do it for you."

Logan stiffened. "Know that the safety of all under my command is my personal responsibility. I don't take this lightly, but I also don't appreciate an outsider threatening me or my Witch Hunters."

Fenris cleared his throat. "I'll escort Ella home. With the increase in demon attacks of late, we all need to be on our guard."

Logan nodded but still stared me down. "Greta, come with me." He finally looked away and I let out a breath.

Fenris mouthed 'It's okay' to me. He must have seen the anxiety written all over my face.

We exchanged goodbyes, Logan and Greta leaving Fenris and I alone in the tavern.

CHAPTER 11

FENRIS

"**W**hat was going on between you and Logan? You both seemed to be getting agitated with one another?" I took a sip of my drink.

"I'm just so sick of men like Andras getting away with everything. He is a horrible person and I understand, it's your job as Witch Hunters, but he is revolting," Ella said as she pinched the bridge of her nose, closing her eyes.

"We have to follow protocol, Ella. Logan will do what has to be done, but it does have to be done right," I explained.

I understood her frustration, but we couldn't relieve Andras of his duties based on Greta's words. I believed her, but that's not how things are done. They need to be done the right way or we'd face a whole world of problems.

"I get that, but you know what Andras is like. You stopped

him from killing me that night... I think you know he's fully capable of murder," she pleaded.

I sighed. "We will get him. I swear it. Just... let Logan do his job."

She shifted in her seat, crossing her arms over her chest. "Fine."

We drifted into an awkward silence for a moment.

"Listen. I'm sorry for the other night. It wasn't my intention to make you feel like I was scared of you," I tried to explain, running my hand through my hair.

"Why wouldn't you let me heal you?" she asked in a hushed tone, I could tell by her expression that she was hurt by what had happened.

"You have to understand how and where I grew up. I'm a Witch Hunter. I didn't even know witches could heal. I just didn't know what to expect."

I couldn't tell her the truth. That when her finger brushed against my hand it did something to me I couldn't explain. I felt something, it was something I should never have felt towards a witch. A spark. Was it her magic or was it more than that?

"Do you trust me?" Ella peered right into my eyes.

I hesitated for a moment and she sighed. "You can sit in here, with an easily healed injury like a coward, or you can be a man, come outside, and I will show you how little you have to fear from me."

She was right. I needed to man up already. I got to my feet. "Lead the way then."

"Excellent," Ella said as she got to her feet too.

I followed her outside, the cold night air biting at my cheeks. She led me to an alleyway where it was dark, and we were hidden from people passing.

Ella reached her hand out to me and waited. I didn't hesitate at all, I placed my hand in hers, welcoming her warmth.

I watched in fascination as she unwrapped my bandage and inspected my wound. It had gotten worse, festering with white pus. The cold air was painful against it, stinging the still open wound.

Ella tsked. "This wouldn't have happened if you just let me fix it the other night." She raised an accusing eyebrow at me, and left me feeling scolded.

"I know, I should have let you heal it," I conceded, refusing to show her that I found her telling me off somewhat endearing. That my heart was skipping a beat as she gently held my hand in hers.

She shrugged. "What's done is done. Let's fix it now."

With her right hand holding my palm up she took her left hand and placed it over the top of my injury. Breathing in and out she closed her eyes, and I watched as her hand glowed, and light trickled from her to me. I could feel her power as it mended my wound. It was as if my skin was being painlessly stitched back together, the warmth from her fire also washing over me. It reminded me of the warmth from an open fire on a freezing cold day.

I couldn't take my eyes off of her as she worked, her face slightly tensed in concentration, her pink lips parted and her breathing steady. It was beautiful, she was beautiful.

The glow faded and Ella opened her eyes. I tore my gaze from her before she caught me staring. I was shocked as I examined my hand. It looked like I was never wounded at all. She smiled when I gasped.

"I've never seen anything like it. Thank you." I gazed into her eyes and smiled back at her. I was in complete awe of her.

"Can all witches heal like this?"

"I can only heal small wounds like your one. My speciality is fire," Ella explained, her tone reflecting her confidence.

She was so comfortable in her magic, yet she was hunted and shamed her entire life for being who she was.

"That's interesting. So, you can use other elements, but you are strongest with only one?" I brushed my hand over my stubble.

This was something Witch Hunters were unaware of, so it was fascinating to learn from the source. The information Ella was so readily giving up was vital knowledge in the fight against witches, learning how best to destroy them, but I simply found myself wanting to know her. I could never bring myself to share such information with my fellow Witch Hunters. I could never see harm come to Ella, or any witch for that matter.

"That's right. We can use all elements but there are limits within the elements we don't specialise in. I can't heal bigger wounds, only small ones that require less magic. It's like a muscle, the more you stretch it, the stronger it gets, but you can only stretch certain muscles so much before they strain. Some witches are stronger than others with the magic they specialise in."

"How do you know what you specialise in?"

"Mostly trial and error. When I was old enough to understand magic, maybe around twelve, Hulda started training me. She encouraged me to test out all the elements to see which one called to me and felt right. I felt capped with all of them except fire. It was as if something stopped me from being able to do more with the other elements. But fire... I can do anything with," Ella explained as we started walking towards the Fraying Forest.

It was like deja vu. Taking her home and making sure she was safe. Not that she needed it. She was strong on her own. Admirable. How could we be so wrong about witches?

"If you can wield fire does that mean fire can't harm you?" I asked.

"Yes, I'm immune to the effects of fire. I can even create a shield. Basically, a witch can invisibly shield their body with their speciality, we wear it like a cloak over our whole body. It comes in handy sometimes. I can also shield myself with live flames which are stronger than the invisible shield but far more dangerous with others around," she answered as we arrived at the entrance to the Fraying Forest. Ella turned to me and smiled.

"Thank you, for trusting me enough to tell me about you," I said.

She blushed. "Just promise you'll never use it against me."

"I won't. You have my word." I turned towards the trees swaying in the night air. "I know you don't feel comfortable with leading me to your home. But would you consider at least letting me get you halfway. Just so I know you're safe?" I asked, hoping she wouldn't say no.

I knew she was strong enough to defend herself, but I wouldn't forgive myself if anything did happen to her because I didn't muster the courage to ask. I also found myself wanting to spend more time with her, getting to know her. I wasn't ready to leave her presence just yet.

She tapped her finger on her mouth for a moment then said, "okay, fine. But I'm trusting you here."

"I won't betray that trust. I swear it," I said.

Her eyes bore into me for a moment until she finally turned and headed into the forest, moving around the trees. I followed closely behind her, watching the movements. The shadows of animals catching my eyes and the sound of them scurrying about. I found it hard not to stare at her frame in front of me, reminding myself I was supposed to be watching for danger, not the sway of her hips.

We walked for a couple of minutes in mostly darkness, the brightness from the moon being the only light we had. There were movements here and there that made us both jump, but it was the sound from up ahead that drew my attention.

"Did you hear that?" I whispered. "I could have sworn I heard a branch snap."

Ella stopped walking and looked around, focusing.

I heard a grunting noise nearby and by the stunned look on Ella's face, I knew she had heard it too.

"We are not alone," Ella murmured.

She stealthily unsheathed the sword from her back, the motion smooth and practised. I removed my two pistols from the holsters on either side of my hips. There were runic symbols from the scholars embedded on the hilts in red, aiding us in the disposal of witches and demons. Ella's eyes snagged on my pistols, widening as she noticed the runes. Another snapping sound had both our heads whipping to the left, too late. The mottled, knobbly demon paw collided with Ella's jaw, sending her flying. I heard a crack, and I hoped that it wasn't her jaw breaking. I was going to kill this demon for hurting her!

"Ella, are you alright?" I yelled in a panic.

I shot at the demon with my pistol and it fell back against a tree, holding its paw up and screeching. Ella sat up as she massaged her jaw.

"Well, that was rude," she replied, looking over towards the demon.

She must have had a strong grip on her sword because she still held it firmly. I helped her to her feet as I heard the low laugh of the demon.

"Pathetic humans," it bellowed as it regained its strength.

The silver markings on its gigantic, lion shaped body glowed then it suddenly disappeared.

"Shit, where did it go?" Ella breathed.

"It's a bloody Crane Demon. It's gone invisible."

"How the hell do we kill an invisible demon?" Ella cried out.

I felt a rush of wind beside me and Ella brought her sword down. Another roar broke through the air as Ella hit it.

The demon lost its invisibility for a moment and started barrelling towards me but before I could react, a ball of flame appeared from the corner of my eye. It hit the Crane Demon's abdomen and made it fall back, hitting its head on the forest floor. It didn't stop the demon, it immediately got to its feet and smiled. The markings started to glow again.

"Brace yourself. It's going invisible," I yelled.

"What do we do?" she yelled back as the demon disappeared from sight.

"Throw your fireballs around and I'll shoot my pistol." I was unsure what it would accomplish against a Crane Demon, but I was hoping at best we'd land a few hits.

"I have a better plan."

Ella raised her two hands in front of her face and started moving around in a circle. Fire began to surround both of us like a flaming shield covering us in all directions. Exactly how she said it would. It was both terrifying and beautiful the amount of magic she seemed to possess. She said fire was her speciality but it was thrilling to see how easily it came to her.

My mouth fell open as I watched. "This is incredible," I muttered.

"Just be careful. Remember what I said, this live shield is more dangerous. Don't get too close to its edges. It'll burn your skin off in mere seconds."

"Noted," I said, clearing my throat.

The demon grunted towards my right but I still couldn't see it. I shot one of my pistols, but it ricocheted off a tree.

"Dammit," I cursed under my breath.

Ella conjured smaller fireballs and started throwing them over our shield in all directions, being careful to avoid trees and anything that could set the whole forest alight.

"Where the hell is it?" I snapped, swiping my hair out of my eyes brusquely.

The Crane Demon didn't seem to want to attack the flaming shield, or it would have done so already.

"Maybe it left?" Ella stopped throwing fireballs.

"Don't take down your shield just yet. It probably wants us to drop our guard."

"We can't..." Ella fell to the ground as if someone or something had tackled her from above before she could finish speaking, her flaming shield disappearing.

I quickly withdrew a dagger that was strapped to my belt, also covered in runes, and slashed above and around Ella. My dagger met resistance, sinking through invisible layers of skin and sinew. Black ichor oozed out of the air. A trail of the stinking, thick blood was running away and as it grew closer to a tree, the Crane Demon came into sight, its invisibility no longer able to save it. The runes on my dagger worked to block the demon's power. The cut I had made was deep on its back.

Ella sprang back into action, launching herself at the demon.

She held out her hands as she got close and fire emerged from them, engulfing the demon. Its piercing scream reverberated through the trees. It was over within minutes, the demon's burnt carcass lying on the ground. The smell of burnt demon flesh permeated the air, making me feel ill.

I looked over at Ella just as she collapsed to the forest floor.

CHAPTER 12

MARELLA

"**A**re you okay?" Fenris ran over and dropped to his knees beside me.

"I think... My head. I feel weak and my head hurts. Need to get to Hulda," I managed to dribble the words out.

"I don't know where you live, Ella." Fenris' voice was panicked.

"Keep walking south-east. The wards will drop when they sense that I'm outside of them." I felt dizzy and like I was going to throw up.

"But won't they still be invisible to me?"

"Not if you're touching me." I forced out, trying to hang on to consciousness.

He brushed hair out of my face. "Please don't die on me," he choked out.

"I've seen how I die and this isn't it." I was so delirious, I had no idea whether I said those words out loud or just thought them.

His jaw tensed and his eyes widened, I had my answer. "What are you talking about?" he asked.

"That Scree demon... it gave me a vision of my death," I tried to speak but I felt so weak.

He placed a finger over my mouth, the warmth filling me and sending a shock down my spine. "Save your energy."

He picked me up and cradled me in his arms then started jogging as fast as he could with me in his arms. My head wobbled from side to side and throbbed viciously.

His eyes drifted down to my hands as he ran. "Your magic is intense."

"You're not still frightened, are you?" I whimpered.

"Not at all. It was... mesmerising. I want to learn more about you... about your magic."

Why did I feel like if I opened up to him, I could trust that he'd keep my secrets? I couldn't deny that something about him drew me in. If he wanted to, he could have turned me in by now or even killed me. He could have allowed the two demons we'd fought together to kill me. He could have let Andras kill me. But he didn't. That had to all count for something.

"Why are you different? I just can't wrap my head around a Witch Hunter not trying to kill me," I asked, my breathing becoming shallow.

"I could never hurt you, Ella." His face was serious. I knew he meant it.

I reached up to touch his face, the contact causing me to falter for a moment and inhale a sharp breath. As quick as I had done it, I pulled my hand back and placed my head against his collarbone as we approached the cottage, my home.

The ward dropped and everything came into view.

Did I think it was a good idea to invite Fenris into my home? Probably not. But I knew he wouldn't hurt me or turn me in, so I felt safe doing so. I also knew that I needed him. I felt so weak, my head pounded in my skull. I wouldn't have been able to get to Hulda without him. I could have very well been left for dead between the trees.

With me still in his arms he manoeuvred around and knocked on the door loudly. My vision was starting to dim.

I heard footsteps then Hulda opened the door, her mouth falling open.

"What on Earth is going on and who are you?" her tone was laced with worry.

"Forgive me. I'm Fenris. Ella has suffered a head injury. Please, help her."

Hulda moved to the side and let Fenris walk in. She shut the door behind her then led him to my room where he gently laid me on my bed.

"Move aside," Hulda said to Fenris.

I felt Hulda's hands against my head and felt the warmth radiate through my skull. It felt like my brain was being given a comforting hug.

After a moment, Hulda dropped her hands and I felt well enough to sit up in my bed. Her magic always impressed me with the speed and concentration you was able to muster.

I peered up at Hulda who was now eyeing Fenris, her lips thinned and her arms crossed.

Uh oh.

"Care to tell me what's going on?" She glanced from me to Fenris.

"You have nothing to fear from me, I swear it. I won't let any harm come to either of you," Fenris explained.

"Is that right? Who are you anyway?" Hulda asked.

Fenris gulped as sweat trickled down his brow. "Well... as you know, my name is Fenris and I'm a Witch Hunter."

"Excuse me?" Hulda scoffed, alarm crossing her features.

"Please, I don't want to hurt either of you. I just wanted to make sure Ella was okay." He cleared his throat. "I'll leave you both alone now."

"I'm sorry, I can't let you leave."

"Hulda, it's fine. He's fine," I tried to reason with her.

"We will figure this mess out in the morning. Fenris, I suggest you sleep out on the couch tonight and I'll see you both in the morning. I have to go sleep off the energy I just expelled." Hulda walked out of my bedroom and waved her hands in front of the windows, back door and front door. Her charm bracelet activating the effects of the horseshoes above the openings.

"What's she doing?" Fenris asked.

"She just made sure you can't leave."

"What do you mean?" he asked, a hint of fear in his voice.

"If you try to walk through the doorways or climb out the windows, the wards will burn you alive," I said matter-of-factly.

The look on his face almost made me burst out laughing. It was a look of pure horror.

"Excellent." Fenris dragged his hand through his hair.

"Listen, she's not going to hurt you. I won't let her anyway. Go get some rest and we will talk in the morning," I said, laying down.

He nodded and left the room, shutting the door behind him.

It didn't take me long at all to fall asleep, the exhaustion of yet another battle taking over me.

***

When I woke the next morning I walked out of my room to find Fenris sitting at the kitchen table, his head in his hands.

"How did you sleep?" I asked as I sat beside him.

"Horribly. How about you?" He lifted his head and his eyes peered into mine. They were bloodshot and droopy.

"Not so well either."

"Ella, you said something yesterday. I haven't been able to get it out of my head all night, I couldn't sleep because of it." He rubbed his eyes. "You said that you had a vision of your death. What happened?" Fenris asked gently.

"I haven't told anyone this," I started. "When you saved me from Andras that night, the Scree Demon I had fought just beforehand gave me a vision after my magic and its power collided. It showed me how I'm going to die. My death will happen here in this cottage, by Lilith." I caressed my arms as goosebumps made their way onto my skin.

"Wait, the Demon Queen? Why would she want to kill you? How much time do you have?" Fenris fired question after question, clearly distressed by this information.

"I still felt young, so it won't be too far away. Everything was blurry so I couldn't see too much but I knew it was Lilith. I would recognise that long, red hair no matter how blurry it was."

Fenris was silent for a moment then finally glanced towards me. "What are you going to do?"

"There's nothing I can do. I'm living on borrowed time." I

shrugged but my heart was pounding.

"Well...we have to try something. There has to be something." Fenris got to his feet and paced the room nervously. He pounded a fist on the table, cursing under his breath.

"You should know as well as I do that you can't change a Scree Demon's vision. I just want to help as many people as I can while I'm still alive to do so," I sighed and got to my feet, moving towards the kitchen window and gazing out at the world.

The sun was just peeking over the horizon and the trees surrounding the cottage swayed gently in the wind. I thought about the fact that I may never see or feel any of it again. The cold air against my face or a warm hug from Hulda, the taste and smell of her cooking. I didn't want to die, but it couldn't be stopped.

"There has to be something we haven't learnt that can help. I'll have the scholars research Scree Demons, I'll search the library in the castle."

"Why do you care so much if I die? You're a Witch Hunter." I turned back around to face him and saw the hopeful look in his eyes.

"I think we've established by now that none of that matters. There's more to you than the fact you're a witch. You're a person, Ella. A good person. I care what happens to you."

"I won't stop you chasing answers, if that's what you want, Fenris. But I have to come to terms with it. I can't change the future, it's done, it's set in stone." I looked away from him, down at the ground.

"No! I won't accept that. I won't let you die." He walked towards me and put his finger on my chin, bringing my face up to look into his eyes. "I refuse to let you die."

His touch and words sent chills down my spine. He cared for me even though he barely knew me. He was a good man with a heart of gold. I really didn't want him to waste his time looking for answers that weren't there, but it warmed my heart to know he wanted to. That maybe more was happening between us. A witch and a Witch Hunter, who would have thought.

"So, do you know if Hulda will let me out any time soon?" He smirked and moved away, his hand dropping to his side.

"Our magic takes a lot out of us. She will wake soon and let you out."

"I don't suppose you could let me out?"

"And deal with the wrath of Hulda? No thanks." I laughed. "I'm kidding. But unfortunately only she can break her own wards."

He sighed and moved away, taking a seat at the kitchen table again. "That first night I saw you, when I saved you from Andras, I felt something. Like maybe it was my fate to save you. Maybe this is the same thing, Ella. Maybe I am fated to save you again."

I blushed. "Maybe." I wasn't confident, but I wouldn't stand in his way.

"So, does Hulda know about all of this?" Fenris asked.

"I don't want to worry her." I bit my lip.

"You've been trying to deal with this on your own? Ella, you need to let people help you... let Hulda help you... let me help you."

"I just... I don't want to be a burden on the people I love." I shrugged my shoulders, trying to play it off as though it was no big deal.

Fenris saw right through me and shook his head. "Dammit, Ella. You aren't. Why would you even think that?"

"I just don't want to cause unnecessary panic that could be avoided."

"You should tell her soon," Fenris scolded.

After a moment of silence, he cracked his knuckles, got to his feet, and stretched.

Hulda's door opened and she walked out, looking between us both. "What are you two talking about?"

"Fenris was just asking if you were going to let him leave or if you'd kill him," I quickly said before Fenris could tell her what we had really been talking about. I chuckled to replace some of the earlier tension.

Neither Fenris nor Hulda looked impressed with my joke. Fenris bit his lip and Hulda narrowed her eyes at me.

"Do you trust him, Ella?" Her eyes searched mine.

I didn't hesitate. "Yes, I do. He won't hurt us."

She nodded. "Fine. You may leave. But if anything ever happens to Ella I will personally make it my life's mission to destroy you."

Hulda went around the house and took down all the wards keeping Fenris locked inside. When she was done she opened the front door, gesturing for Fenris to leave.

He looked towards me. "I guess I better get going. I'll keep you updated on any information I find. I'll be at the tavern or around it every night if you ever need to talk. Just... stay safe, okay?"

"Don't worry about me too much. I'll be fine." I half smiled.

He frowned at that, and I shrugged.

"If only it were that easy," he mumbled. "I'll catch up with you later, Ella," he said as he walked out the front door.

CHAPTER 13

FENRIS

awn brought with it cold, rain and wind. It was pelting down as I quickly ran from the carriage to the church doors to start my day. I was on an important mission, and I wasn't going to stop until I found something to save Ella. The first thing I planned to do was to find Greta. She was someone Ella trusted and I knew she would have the utmost discretion with the situation.

I searched the library, but I couldn't find her amongst any of the shelves or at the tables. I searched her living quarters and still couldn't find her. I was about to give up and go ask Logan if he'd seen her, when I glanced around an open hallway and saw her familiar blonde bun, conversing with two other scholars. The rain against the windows was drowning out their voices, so I had to speak loudly to get her attention.

"Hey Greta," I raised my voice over the noise.

She jumped when she heard me and glanced over. "Fenris, What's going on? You look drenched."

"I don't recommend going outside right now." I smirked.

"I wasn't planning on it, but thank you." She peered back at the other scholars and waved goodbye then walked towards me. "What can I do for you?"

"I need your help with Ella." I got straight to the point.

Her face instantly turned to worry. "What's wrong? Is she alright?" Greta motioned me over to the side of the hallway so we were out of the way and could talk somewhat freely.

"I'm so sorry to put this on you," I nervously brushed the hair out of my face.

Greta's eyebrows furrowed as she frowned. "You're scaring me."

"We did get caught up with ... something, but she's fine now."

"Oh, I'm glad she's okay," Greta sighed.

"I need to speak to you about something but I need you to swear to me that this stays between us?" My heart was racing in my chest.

Greta rubbed her arms. "You have my word, Fenris. If I can help Ella I will."

"Ella is ... well, she's a witch." I waited for her shocked expression but it never came. "You knew?"

She hesitated a moment as her eyes peered down at the ground. "I've known ever since she rescued me from the demon worshippers. That's how she saved me. She used her fire magic."

"You didn't turn her in?" I wasn't surprised somehow.

"Of course not! She saved my life, why would I ruin hers?"

"Fair point," I conceded.

"Why haven't you turned her in? You are a Witch Hunter." She narrowed her eyes.

"It's a long story that I'm sure one of us will tell you someday, but right now I need your help to save her."

Greta took a deep breath in and out. "Okay, what do you need?"

"We need your help to find out information about a Scree Demon and their visions. If they can be altered."

"Have you come across a Scree Demon?" Greta tilted her head.

"Yes, we did. This was a demon Ella fought by herself not long ago. It triggered a vision." I looked around to make sure nobody was too close.

"What was in this vision?"

"Ella saw the moment she... Well, she saw when she's going to die."

"Oh." Greta covered her mouth.

"I want to prevent it from happening, if we can."

"When does it happen?"

"She isn't exactly sure, but she said she knows she's young. So I'd say soon," I explained solemnly.

"What can I do to help?" she immediately offered.

"You're familiar with the church library. Can you try and find anything relating to a Scree demon's visions?"

"Of course. Whatever you need. Whatever she needs, I'm here."

I placed my hand on her shoulder and she nodded in understanding before turning and rushing down the hall and out of sight. That was my first matter of business for the day settled. Now I had to make my way to the castle to see if I could find anything in their library that could help.

***

When I entered the library, I was glad to find it empty apart from the librarian and his assistant. They were sitting at a desk in the far-right corner chatting about some literature they discovered. There were so many books I had no idea where to even begin, it was overwhelming and I was worried the task would take days. I decided to start the opposite way from the librarians, so they didn't ask questions.

I searched and skimmed for hours, only going through books that had any relevance. Demons, destiny, prophecies, and I was still coming up blank. I let out a frustrated groan and jumped when I felt a hand on my back.

"Why are you reading '*Fate and Prophecies*' by Fred Murr?" Lyra asked as I shut the book.

"No reason. Why are you creeping up behind people?" I raised my eyebrows.

She laughed. "You can only be creeped up on if you're not focused on your surroundings. As a Witch Hunter, doesn't that kind of go against your training?"

"Touché," I said as I rolled my eyes.

"So... why are you reading that book?" she asked again.

"You're very nosy today."

"I'm bored! I'm being forced to sit here in this castle all day and night. I need to do something! I need adventure!" She paused for a moment. "So... why are you reading that book?"

"If I tell you then you have to promise to keep it to yourself."

She scoffed. "Do you not trust me, Fen?"

"I mean it. We are talking about someone's life."

Her eyes went wide. "Alright! I Promise I won't say anything. You can always trust me, Fen."

I gave her a similar spiel I gave Greta and watched as her face turned from worry to motivation. We kept looking over at the librarians every now and again but they were too immersed in their own conversation to care.

Lyra suddenly grabbed a book from the shelf and started perusing it.

"What are you doing?" I glanced from her to the book.

"Finding a solution, why? What are you doing?" She smirked and placed her face further into the book.

I relented. "Fine. I have already covered this area." I gestured towards the three bookshelves I had already gone through. "Thank you... for helping."

She nodded with a smile, put the book back that I had already read and moved towards some book shelves closer to the librarians. She, at least, wouldn't get questioned.

I had no idea how much time had passed but my eyes were starting to get sore and heavy from reading so much. I was rubbing them when Lyra came up behind me and made me jump for the second time.

"I think I found something," she said excitedly.

I turned quickly and saw the book she was holding. There was text on the left page and a picture on the right. She handed it to me, and I studied it. The picture was a drawing of a demon holding a sword.

"The book says this is the Sword of Fatum, Latin for destiny. It can change someone's fate," Lyra explained.

I looked up at her from the book. "Lyra, this is incredible. This could save her. This could prevent Ella's death."

Lyra's brows furrowed. "The only problem is it doesn't say where it is or if it is even real. It could very well just be a story. I've also never seen this demon before in any texts I've ever read... have you?"

I shook my head and joined her concern.

"It also doesn't say how to use it. I don't think we can stab Ella with it to save her from being killed. That would defeat the purpose of needing the sword." Lyra sighed.

It felt like we had half the information and no idea how to retrieve the rest. "So where do we go from here? How can we find out if this sword is real or if it's just another myth? I can ask a scholar I trust, Greta, if she has ever seen this demon in her studies."

"That's a good idea. You do that and I'll see if I can get any information out of the librarians."

"Be careful, Lyra. Because of who Ella is, we can't trust anyone."

"Oh, Fen. It's like you don't even know me! I'll have them wrapped around my little finger in no time! They won't suspect a thing!" Her teeth were showing with how wide her grin was.

"Inconspicuous you mean? Let's not forget that you're stuck in this castle because you got caught," I smiled.

She nudged me in the side and smiled back. "If you're done being... well, you, I'm going to go talk to them. Be careful, yourself."

With that she walked away and I shut the book. I had to make it back to Greta and show her before I went to Ella. It had been a long day and I was really starting to feel it. Instead of sleeping I studied all day and I knew it was going to bite me tonight. I was just grateful I had the night off.

I made my way back to the church where Logan was standing out the front talking to a few of our fellow Witch Hunters.

"Fenris, are you ready for tonight?" he asked, a smile on his face.

"What's happening tonight?" I raised an eyebrow at him.

"It's our night off and I feel like we haven't had time to talk just about trivial things in a while."

"You know what, that actually sounds good right about now." Despite being tired, I knew I needed a night to decompress from everything.

"Walk with me?" Logan gestured towards the tavern and we both began to walk. "You seem troubled lately."

"Do I?" I tried to make my voice sound neutral but it came out higher.

"Your mind seems to be wandering like it used to when we were younger."

I looked over to him. "How do you know when my mind wanders?"

He laughed. "Fenris, I've known you my entire life. The only person who knows you better than me is Princess Lyra." He stopped walking. "You know you can talk to me ... about anything."

I looked away from him and started walking again. "I know that. You're my best friend, after all. But it is nothing."

I felt horrible that I was keeping things from him. It didn't feel right, I owed him so much more than this after everything we'd been through together. But there was no way I could share this with him, confide in him. Even friendships had limits.

"So ... You and Greta seem closer," I changed the subject.

Logan grinned. "I like her Fenris. I really like her."

"What about Lyra?" I teased and he shoved me.

"Princess Lyra and I will never work, I know that. I think it's time I moved on from that crush, don't you?"

I nodded. "I think you're right."

We eventually reached the tavern and entered. The first

person I saw was Ella, seated alone. I peered around and saw Greta at the bar. She looked towards Logan and I, smiled then turned back to the barmaid and started talking to them again.

"I saw that smile, Logan," I teased.

"Shut up!" He shoved me as we both made our way over to the table.

CHAPTER 14

MARELLA

I sat at the edge of my bed, watching as the rain poured down against my bedroom window. I dreaded walking out of my room. I had decided I was going to listen to Fenris' advice and tell Hulda but the thought of doing so made me want to be sick. I didn't want to worry her, and I knew she was going to constantly do so the second I had this conversation with her. But the truth was, I had no idea how much longer I had left, and I wanted to make sure I accomplished as much as I could before my end came. I also felt like it was better for Hulda to know now than to deal with the sudden grief of my death. I would want to know if it was her, forewarned is best in cases like these.

I sighed and walked out my door. The smell of freshly cooked bacon instantly wafted up my nose. The thought that I would never eat Hulda's cooking again after my death shattered me.

My stomach felt like it was knotted. "I need to talk to you," I said to Hulda, my voice weak.

I had to lead with that, or I knew I wouldn't be able to go through with it. Hulda turned around, her eyebrows raised and her mouth in a thin line. She was worried, the exact thing I wanted to prevent.

"Ella... what's going on? Are you alright?" She came towards me and gestured for me to sit next to her at the table.

"I don't want you to freak out but I need to tell you this."

"Ella, you're worrying me, what's going on?"

"That fight I had with the Scree Demon. I was given a vision."

"What's going to happen?" she asked when I paused.

"The vision was... well, it was of my death." I took a deep breath after getting that out.

Hulda gasped and pulled me into a hug. "Oh, sweet child. Tell me everything."

We spent the morning talking it over. I cried, she cried and I told her I had come to terms with it even though I wasn't sure I had. When I told her it was Lilith a look of fury crossed her face but it was gone in an instant and she got to her feet.

"You're certain it was Lilith?" she asked, her body stiffening beside me.

"The image was blurry, but you can't mistake her red hair. Why... what is it?"

"Nothing. I just wonder if maybe we can avoid having to deal with her after... after what happened to your parents. Maybe we can reason with her. Give her something she wants. Or maybe we should leave the cottage, go somewhere else." Hulda appeared uncomfortable, shifting in her seat.

I interrupted her train of thought. "No way. I am not going

to make any kind of deal with such evil. If it is going to happen, then I need to accept it. I want my death to mean something. I want to know that I've dealt as critical a blow to the demons as I possibly can before I'm gone. Besides, what could she possibly want that we have?" I questioned.

Hulda bit her lip and sweat formed across her forehead. I knew she was worried and scared but nothing was worth trying to reason with Lilith. I would rather not put my family and friends in the firing line.

"Well then, let's put fresh wards up around the cottage to at least try and prevent her from seeking out our home." Hulda had quickly veered the conversation away. She got to her feet and moved away before I could talk any further on the matter.

Protection was futile. Lilith would find this cottage no matter what, it was in the vision. But it made Hulda feel better, so I went along with it.

We grabbed a basket and started filling it with the items we kept in storage for warding. Things like stones, rabbits feet, horseshoes and preserved four leafed clovers. They all helped keep a home protected when placed correctly.

We made our way outside, the rain still holding strong. This task was going to be more difficult in such dreary weather.

We started walking around the cottage, digging small holes in the ground every now and again, burying an item each time. Thankfully the cottage had eaves along the roof that covered us as we walked around.

We had finally finished warding the house then branched out further to establish where we wanted the wards to end, the rain drenching us in seconds.

We were about ten feet from the cottage then started doing the same, going around the house keeping this distance, digging holes and burying the items.

By the time we finished securing the wards, it was the end of the day and we were both shivering with goosebumps down our arms.

Hulda healed some dead trees to try and conceal the cottage more before we finally made our way inside. We were both so exhausted and sore from it all but it made Hulda feel less anxious and that's what mattered to me. I was so glad when Hulda said she would make us a nice, warm stew. I hadn't noticed how hungry I was until we had stopped working our magic.

We finished the meal just as the sun was setting and I told Hulda I had to go into town. The rain had finally stopped, leaving behind a wet forest floor.

"Please be safe, Ella," Hulda said, putting her hand on my face.

"I will. Don't worry about me. Nothing will happen to me out there, remember?"

She sighed. "That does not make me worry about you any less, dear."

***

I walked into the tavern and immediately spotted Greta sitting at our usual spot. She was concentrating on a book with an ale in her hand. I walked over and took a seat but she was so immersed she didn't notice me.

"What are you reading?" I asked.

She jumped slightly, spilling some ale on her book, but she glanced up and smiled. "Ella, I'm so glad to see you. I've been studying all day."

"What have you been studying?" I asked.

"Fenris told me about your vision and asked me to help out."

"Excuse me. He what?" My eyes widened.

Greta flinched. "Was I not supposed to know?"

"Nobody was supposed to know. I didn't want everyone worrying about me," I said, raising my voice slightly before reigning it in.

"I'm glad he told me. You saved me, now I get to help figure out how to save you. I won't be sorry for that."

I softened. "You don't have to be sorry about anything, Greta. Someone else does." I crossed my arms and fell back against my chair. "So, what have you learnt then?" I asked, giving in to curiosity.

She nodded and closed the book. "From what I can tell so far, the Scree Demon's visions are absolute. They come true no matter how much you try to avoid the outcome. I'm sorry, Ella. I wish I had better news."

"Stop saying sorry. I appreciate you looking but I knew nothing would come of it. If I'm destined to die, I just need to accept it."

She gave a half smile and gave me the rest of her ale. "You look like you need this. I'll order us more."

As I watched her head towards the bar, I saw Fenris enter but he wasn't alone. He was with Logan, and when they spotted me, they made their way over. They both took a seat and as they did Fenris noticed Greta's book on the table. He quickly turned it over before Logan could see.

"What are you two doing here?" I asked, avoiding eye contact with Fenris.

"It's our night off so we decided to head out. How's your night?" Logan was the one to answer. He seemed less hostile than before. Maybe it was because he was off duty.

"Just catching up with Greta." I smiled.

Greta reappeared with a tray filled with glasses of ale.

"I saw you both come in so I decided to shout you. Next round is on you, Fenris." She took a seat next to me and handed the glasses out.

"I'm happy to get the next one." Logan smiled at her, and I caught her smiling back.

"Ella... do you mind if we go for a walk?" Fenris asked, already getting to his feet.

I gritted my teeth. "Of course not. I was about to ask you the same thing." I looked at Greta. "I'll be right back."

We headed outside, the air cold against my skin, making me shiver.

I turned around to face Fenris when we were far enough away from the tavern. "Why would you tell Greta about my vision?"

He appeared taken aback. "I told you I would ask the scholars to research Scree Demons."

"I didn't know that also included telling one my secret." I crossed my arms.

"I thought Greta was your friend?"

"She is. Which is exactly why I would rather her not know. You and Hulda are enough to deal with."

"Deal with? What's that supposed to mean?" He paused for a moment. "You told Hulda. Ella, that's great." He smiled then his lips turned thin, as though he remembered we were arguing.

"Have you told anyone else, Fenris?" I chastised.

He rubbed the back of his neck. "I did tell Princess Lyra. I'm sorry but she caught me researching and wanted to help."

I threw my hands up in the air and scoffed. "Why don't you

just tell the whole world. In fact, go into the tavern and tell Logan I'm a witch. I'm sure he'll love that and then maybe I can avoid Lilith anyway because no doubt Logan will kill me first."

"Ella, calm down. I'm sorry, alright. I just want to help." His eyes were glistening.

I sighed. "I understand you want to help, Fenris and I am so grateful for that but this was my secret and there was a reason I was keeping it that way." I grabbed his hand and he gazed up into my eyes. "Thank you for caring, for helping me. Just... Please don't tell anyone else."

"I won't. I swear it."

I started to shiver again as the cool air bit harder. Fenris looked down at my arms then started rubbing them with his hands. "You're freezing."

My teeth began to chatter. "I'll be fine."

Fenris took off his coat and draped it over my shoulders. It was big and warm, and I was instantly grateful as it shielded me from the chilly night air. As I took a breath in I could smell the subtle scent of him on his coat. He smelt of musk and ale. It was hypnotising.

After a moment of silence where neither one of us knew how to proceed, Fenris finally spoke. "We may have found something." I noted the excitement in his voice.

"That cannot be possible... my fate is sealed. The threads of destiny cannot be altered, nor can we trick them. What will be, will be." I pulled his coat tighter around me. "I spoke to Greta inside and she confirmed it."

"Princess Lyra and I found an item in a book called The Sword of Fatum. The only problem is, we have no idea where it is or how to find it."

"What is The Sword of Fatum? What does it do?"

"It's a sword that can change someone's fate. We can use it to change yours." Fenris' eyes lit up.

"What do we do now then?" I refused to let that tiny spark of hope inside of me take flame. This could all very well lead to a dead end.

"I'll speak with Lyra tomorrow to see if she found any new information. This is promising, Ella. This could potentially save your life." He was excited, but I didn't feel like I could mirror that, not yet.

We had no idea whether this was just a story or whether it was true. If it was true, where was the sword and how was it going to help anyway? So many questions needed to be answered and I had no idea if we would gain the knowledge in time. For all I knew it could happen tomorrow.

Fenris placed his hand on my back and the pressure of it through the jacket sent a shiver down my spine. I couldn't believe this Witch Hunter was trying to save my life. Why did he care so much? I glanced up at him and saw him smiling down at me. My heart started beating erratically as I smiled back.

"Thank you. For everything. I'm sorry about before," I said.

He took my hand in his and squeezed it. "We better get back inside. I did want to tell Greta what we'd learnt before nightfall, but I didn't catch up with her in time. I'll leave with Logan so you can talk to her."

I hesitated a moment then pulled him back. "Wait, before you go I have something for you."

He peered into my eyes and gave me his full attention. "What is it?"

It was something I'd been contemplating for a while now.

He'd saved me several times and with my vision I knew I'd die inside my cottage. I wanted him to be able to get Hulda to safety when it all went down and he couldn't do that if he couldn't find our home.

I handed him a bracelet with an amethyst embedded into it. "This should help you locate our cottage. The amethyst is spelled to reveal our home to you."

"Why are you giving this to me?" He took it and turned it around in his hands, studying it.

"Because if anything happens to me I need you to promise you'll help save Hulda."

"Nothing is going to happen to you."

"Please ... just promise me."

"Okay. I promise. But nothing will happen to you." He put the bracelet on then pulled me in, hugging me close. My body tingled at the sensation of his warmth and touch.

"We better get back in there," he said as he pulled away and I nodded, not trusting myself to speak.

We both headed back inside and as we walked over to the table; Greta was laughing. She was leaning into Logan, both of them whispering and Greta had her hand on his shoulder. I wondered if Scholars and Witch Hunters could be together? And what about witches and Witch Hunters? It seemed obscene, but could Fen and I have a future? Was that what I wanted, a future with Fen? Where were these thoughts even coming from? I shook them from my mind.

"Logan, I think it's time we get out of here," Fenris said, gesturing at the door. He moved his glass of ale towards me. "You can have mine. I'll get you both next time."

Logan hesitated for a moment, seeming as though he didn't want to leave Greta, but eventually he and Fenris left, walking out the tavern doors.

"Logan seems lovely when he's not being a jerk," I said as I took a seat.

"He's a nice guy, very funny. He's just very serious when it comes to his job." She changed the subject before I could say more. "What did Fenris talk to you about?"

I explained it all to her except for our argument, she didn't need to know about that. I watched her face fill with excitement at the mention of the sword.

"We can work with this, Ella," Greta clapped her hands together.

"Hopefully we can find it but if not, I want you all to know how grateful I am. Especially since I only really just met you all not long ago and you could get in a lot of trouble for helping a *witch*," I whispered the last word so nobody would hear.

"I will go back to the church right now and start studying. You head home and stay safe, okay?" Greta finished her drink and left the tavern. I followed shortly after and trekked home.

CHAPTER 15

FENRIS

Logan summoned me to his office the next day. He wanted to discuss our meeting with Greta and Ella from the previous night. He was sitting at his desk while I leant against a wall.

"So, what did you and Ella talk about outside?" Logan asked.

I was having trouble trying to think of something to say. "Ah, she wanted to know if we had any updates on Andras." Truth was, I thought Ella was too preoccupied with everything going on right now to worry too much about Andras. I assured her he would be taken care of and I felt like she trusted that.

Logan scoffed. "She needs to keep her nose out of Witch Hunter business."

"She's just worried for her friend." I walked over and took a seat opposite Logan's desk.

"I understand that, but how we handle things is none of her business."

"But it is my business, being that I am a Witch Hunter too and your best friend." I fiddled with a pen on the desk. "Do you have any updates regarding Andras?"

"I have sent him away for a while, to the outskirts of Valdori. I told him we have heard complaints about demons in the area and I wanted him to investigate. He shouldn't be a problem for a while."

"Hopefully we can figure out what to do with him before he gets back." I sighed and Logan nodded.

"So, you and Ella seem to be getting along nicely?"

I blushed. "She's an incredible person. You should really get to know her, she's very strong and resilient."

"Maybe. But it would only be for your sake."

There was a pause then I looked up to see Logan staring out his window to the right.

"What about you and Greta? There was something going on between you two when Ella and I came back in." I smirked. "It'll probably be good for you to focus on something other than your work."

Logan glanced around the room nervously. "Greta is a very smart young woman. I admire how quickly she can adapt to her surroundings and how well she retains information. She's been so fascinated suddenly with Scree Demons." He answered.

My eyes widened at the mention of Scree Demons. "Oh, has she? What has she said about them?"

Logan titled his head and narrowed his eyes. "Why is everyone so interested in Scree Demons lately?"

"Well, I'm more curious after that one that Andras disposed of." I still couldn't believe he claimed that kill as his own but I couldn't come out and say that to Logan.

"I'm sure Greta would be more than happy to talk to you about it, if you're interested."

"I'll ask her next time I see her." I drummed my fingers on the desk.

"What is it?" Logan asked.

"I just wanted you to know that I'm glad you and Greta are getting along. You deserve to be happy."

He tried to hide a smile. "Thank you, Fenris."

Logan had been with women before but he had never been in love or infatuated like he was with Lyra. I knew Lyra didn't feel the same. Not because she told me, but because I knew her like a sister. The last thing on her mind was being tied down to someone. She was a very headstrong person who loved her freedom. Which is why she was losing her mind locked up in that castle. All that aside, I knew Greta would be good for Logan if he kept letting her in, Lyra could never be what Logan needed. As much as I loved Lyra for who she was, Logan needed someone who could ground him.

My thoughts drifted to Ella and how we were going to save her. The Sword of Fatum. There had to be some way of finding it. I knew Logan was big on history so it was a possibility he had heard of it before. I just had no idea how I was going to broach the subject without him becoming suspicious.

"Can I ask you something before I go?" I approached wearily.

"Of course." He rolled his shoulders.

"I was reading in the library with Lyra the other day and we stumbled upon an interesting book. I was wondering if you knew anything about it?" I shifted in my chair.

Logan looked up, interest crossing his features. "Go on."

"It was called the Sword of Fatum. I assume it's just a myth but we found it fascinating."

"Wanting to change your destiny are you, Fenris? Witch Hunter suits you though." He laughed, and I nervously chuckled in response.

"No, not at all. Just found it a compelling story and wanted to see if there was any truth to it. How did you know what it does?"

"I recall Imogen telling us tales of the great sword when I was barely out of swaddling clothes. I used to love those tales, I always thought they were just make-believe stories, but if anyone could help you discern fact from fiction, it would be her. After all, she's lived amongst those books for longer than the King himself."

"Hang on, Imogen told us stories about the sword?" I tilted my head and raised my right eyebrow.

"You don't remember that one? Maybe you weren't paying attention, you had a habit of letting your mind wander." Logan smirked.

"Maybe my mind just isn't as sharp as it used to be."

"Oh, I don't believe that at all." Logan stood. "Listen, I better go file some of these reports that have been sitting on my desk. Just... talk to Immy and see what she says. But I warn you, Fenris... I won't allow you to leave us. You're a Witch Hunter forever." Logan appeared menacing and my stomach dropped. But his expression changed and he winked with a big grin on his face then walked out the door. I still couldn't tell if he was being serious or not.

***

I rode Rhino to the castle and found Imogen in the kitchens

getting lunch ready for the day.

"Miss me?" I asked as I planted myself in front of her while she kneaded dough.

She sighed. "What trouble have you come to cause today?"

"Can't a Witch Hunter come to see his favourite cook?"

She rolled her eyes but smiled. "What can I do for you, Fen?"

"I was talking to Logan, and he said you may know something about the Sword of Fatum?" My heart raced as I asked.

Imogen stopped what she was doing. She wiped her hands on her apron and moved me aside out of earshot of the other kitchen maids. "What do you want with that sword?"

"Nothing... I was just wondering if the story was true?" I was even more nervous now.

"Don't play games with me, Fenris. I'm not a stupid old woman. What do you want with the sword?" she asked again.

"I need it for a friend. I can't say anymore. Please." I brushed my hand through my hair nervously.

"Fenris, you're playing with something dangerous. That sword was created by very powerful beings. It can be risky if used incorrectly," she tried to whisper. "It was crafted in a far away land by a demon named Fatum and his wife, who was a witch. They were both killed before they could ever use it and the sword has been passed around over the years."

I held up my hand. "Wait, the demon's name was Fatum? Meaning destiny in latin?" I was confused now.

"Yes. His name means destiny and he crafted a sword to change his. I assume he found it fitting to name it the Sword of Fatum. Named after himself but also for what the sword was for."

I hesitated. "Do you know where it is?"

Imogen wiped her hands on her apron. "To this day the

sword is rumoured to still be making the rounds. Do you not remember the stories I told you as a young man?" she tsked with impatience.

"The story does sound familiar." I held my chin. "So, it is real?" My eyes went wide.

Imogen shifted on her feet and sighed. "I've said too much." She went to walk away.

I grabbed her arm. "Please, Imogen. Do you know where I can find it?"

She looked at me as though she were studying me then answered. "The last person I know of who possessed it was a fortune teller named Marge. She owns a shop in Hunterville."

"Imogen, I could kiss you. Thank you so much."

She screwed up her face. "You will do no such thing. Now get out of my kitchen."

I went to walk away and she called out to me.

"Please, be careful."

***

As I was heading out of the castle I almost ran into Lyra and Logan.

"Oh Fenris, did you ask Imogen about that sword?" Logan enquired. Lyra furrowed her eyebrows.

"I did. She said it was just a story." I lied to Logan. It made me feel terrible, but I couldn't explain to him why I needed it.

"That's too bad. It would have been interesting if such a thing did exist," Logan answered.

"Listen, Logan. I need to go out of town for a while. Do I have your permission to take leave?" My heart was hammering in my chest.

Logan narrowed his eyes. "Whatever for?" he asked, just as I suspected he would.

Lyra had a confused look planted on her face.

"I can't explain it at the moment, but I just need you to trust me that it is for a good reason. I promise to explain it all to you when I get back."

"I don't know, Fen. The King did give you orders to report your comings and goings to me. I feel he may not be happy if I let you leave." Logan chewed on his bottom lip.

"Hey, if I have to be stuck here, so do you. It wouldn't be fair if you got to leave and I was still tortured with boredom in the castle," Lyra piped in, crossing her arms and pouting.

I waved her off. "Don't be so dramatic, Lyra. You know I wouldn't ask to leave if it wasn't important." I gave her a look that suggested this was urgent.

"Fine, but I expect to hear all about it when you return." Lyra put her hands on her hips.

"Hang on, I haven't even given him permission to leave yet." Logan wrinkled his nose and furrowed his eyebrows.

Lyra slapped him gently on the shoulder. "Your best friend just said this is important. Let him go do what needs to be done. He said he would tell us when he gets back."

Logan rubbed his shoulder, finally coming to a decision after a moment. "Fine. I will let you leave but I want a full explanation the second you return and if anything happens to you I'm blaming the both of you." He glanced between Lyra and I, pointing a finger at both of us.

"Don't blame me, I'm innocent." Lyra shrugged and walked away.

"I swear I will tell you everything," I answered.

Logan nodded. "Stay safe then, Fen." He walked away

towards the castle entrance.

I was about to go back to my bedroom when Lyra came around the corner. "Fen, do you have a moment before you leave? I need you to run an errand for me," Lyra said in a whisper.

"What is it?" I asked warily.

"Theo, Adrian, and Glen have more information. I received a note from them asking to meet, but as you know father won't let me leave the castle. I need you to go see them before you go." Her tone sounded desperate.

"I don't know, Lyra. I really should be going. This is important."

She interrupted me, "What's more important than the survival of our kingdom?"

"Have you relayed any of the information to the King yet?" I gave her a stern look.

"Listen, I swear I'm going to tell him but right now I want to gather more intel," Lyra groaned.

"I really think you should tell him now, Lyra. He won't take kindly to you keeping such knowledge from him."

"Fine, When you come back I will tell him everything. I just wanted to gather enough so he'll feel proud of me, of what I was able to learn," she argued.

"I get that, I really do, but he is the King and this is his kingdom that needs protection. He needs to know," I said, a little more firmly than I intended to.

She sighed. "You're right... I know you are."

"Okay, I will go and be back before nightfall then you will tell the King everything."

She rolled her eyes. "Fine, I will. But before you go... what was that all about with Logan?"

I whispered, "We have a lead on the sword."

"Oh my god, that's amazing!" Lyra shouted, and I shushed her. "Sorry, that's exciting news. Well, you better get moving so you can be on your way."

"I'll see you soon," I said as I raced out the castle doors and retrieved Rhino from the stables.

I rode as fast as I could without raising suspicion and made it to the triplet's house in no time. Glen opened the door for me and let me in.

"Sorry, Princess Lyra couldn't make it, but she sent me. She has been ordered by the King to stay within the castle until further notice," I explained, taking a seat in their living room where we had met before. Glen and Adrian sat opposite me.

"That's fine, Fenris. Princess Lyra told us that if there was any reason she couldn't come she would send either you or George," Glen said.

I nodded. "So, what have you learnt?"

"Theo left this morning to go back across enemy lines. We have some news regarding King Neldor," Adrian started.

Glen picked up the conversation, "We discovered that he's working with Lilith, the Demon Queen."

My mouth flew open, "Wait... are you serious? You're kidding. Why would she help them?"

"Your guess is as good as ours. He must have something she wants, otherwise I don't see why she would bother inserting herself in a human war," Adrian answered, shrugging his shoulders.

"Do you think they will attack Crayton?" My heart was racing.

"One of the maids we regularly talk to told us they are readying for an attack." Adrian rubbed the back of his neck.

"Any ideas yet when they are planning to strike?" I was

hoping it wouldn't be soon.

Glen sighed, "We are still working on that. Theo is going to come back in the next couple of days to let us know if he found anything more. He can be quite charming with Neldor's maids so we are hoping to get information from them to pass on to you."

"I will take this information to Princess Lyra now and let her know you'll be in touch. She gave me this to give to you." I handed Glen another bag of coins just like last time. He put the bag in his pocket.

"Please let King Aldric know that we are grateful for his ongoing protection and coin for our help." Adrian patted me on the back.

So, they weren't aware that Lyra wasn't telling King Aldric this information. I guess if I was in their position and Lyra told me the King didn't know, I would seek him out and tell him myself. I would have to convince her that keeping this information from the King was too harmful to the kingdom.

I said my goodbyes and walked out the door, mounting Rhino for the third time that day and heading back to the castle to relay the information to Lyra before I had to leave.

***

"I just don't understand what Lilith has to do with any of this," Lyra said, leaning against her bedroom door.

I had given her all the information and she was just as shocked as I was to learn about the Demon Queen's involvement. She rubbed her eyes and walked to her desk, taking a seat.

"I had some time to think on my way back, maybe King

Neldor has some kind of magical device she wants. Lilith usually wouldn't bother with human squabbles, we all know she sits on her throne and gets her higher demons to do all her dirty work."

"Precisely, which is why it's so confusing." Lyra rubbed her temples. "Maybe King Neldor is going to take Lilith as his wife." She chuckled.

"Could you imagine marrying a demon." I scoffed. "Or maybe she's just using him to take over the world."

Lyra grumbled. "Well, thank you for helping me, Fen. I knew I could count on you. I expect to hear all about your trip when you get back. Stay safe, okay?" Lyra got to her feet and gave me a hug and a smile.

"I promise I will," I said before leaving her room.

I practically ran out the castle doors. The sun was close to setting, but I could see several stars in the sky already. I had to go visit Ella and update her on the search for the sword. I would head to the church first to write the request for leave out, pack and let Greta know where we were going. Then I was going to make my way into the Fraying Forest and straight to Ella's cottage. I was hopeful that we'd found the answer to save her.

CHAPTER 16

MARELLA

I was alone in the cottage enjoying a mug of hot chocolate, when I heard a knock at the door. I jumped in my seat, spilling the hot liquid all over the table. My heart was thundering in my chest as I walked over to the door and grasped the handle. What if this was it? What if Lilith or one of her demons was here to get me?

I yanked the door open with my sweaty palm and let out a shaky breath when I saw Fenris. He was wearing the amethyst bracelet around his wrist and had a big bag attached to his back.

Did I really think Lilith would knock if she came here? I huffed out a laugh at the ridiculous thoughts.

Fenris frowned. "What's wrong, you look as white as a ghost?"

"Forgive me for being a little on edge when alone in the place of my imminent death." I smirked but I could still feel my heart racing in my chest.

"It may not be so imminent, Ella," he said as I closed the door behind him, moving back into the kitchen.

"What do you mean?" I started cleaning the spilt hot chocolate, it was a nervous habit of mine to clean.

He stopped me and pulled me towards him, brushing hair behind my ear then dropping his arm, his touch sending chills down my spine. "I have some news regarding the sword."

I cleared my throat, doing my best to ignore the intimate way he was touching me. "I'm hoping it's good news."

"I have a lead of where it could be or at least where it last was." He dropped his bag and leant it against the table.

"This all seems too convenient. I'm not sure whether to believe this could actually be real or not," I said sceptically.

"I can understand not wanting to get your hopes up, but we have to try. Follow every lead possible."

I nodded. "When do we leave then?"

"We could leave in the morning when the sun rises, if you're fine with that."

"I'm okay with that. Thank you, Fenris. This means a lot to me." I smiled.

"Sometimes you just need people beside you to support you and show you that giving up is not an option." He took my hand in his, gently caressing it. I'm sure he meant it to be supportive, but his touch sent sparks flying up my arm and into my chest.

"I appreciate that, I really do."

"Do you know what you're going to tell Hulda about us leaving?" Fenris asked.

"I'm not sure, I don't know if she'd let me go or not if I told her. She's very protective of me." I was finding it very hard to focus on anything other than his soft lips moving, his eyes gazing into mine. My breath caught.

"Where is Hulda by the way?" he asked, looking around the cottage.

"She's out tending to some of the townsfolk."

"Wait, people in town know that you're witches?" His eyes widened.

"Only a select few know for sure, people we've known for years and trust," I explained.

"I had no idea there were people in town who even knew witches."

"There's still a lot you don't know about my kind." I smirked and he smiled back.

He dropped my hand to move his bags, and I instantly missed the warmth of him.

Thinking about what I would say to Hulda made me realise I couldn't confront her right now about this. I couldn't tell her I was leaving with a Witch Hunter. She may have let Fenris leave and keep his life before but I didn't think she'd take nicely to me going on a trip with him.

"Actually, do you mind if we leave now?"

Fenris tilted his head and furrowed his eyebrows. "Are you sure you don't want to wait for Hulda?"

"I think we should leave quietly. I fear telling her will just cause more problems than we need. I'll go pack and meet you out the front in a moment."

"Hulda won't show up in the meantime, right?" Fenris rubbed his cheek.

I giggled. "Hulda is usually out until late afternoon when she goes to town to heal. You'll be fine."

He scoffed. "I wasn't worried for me."

"Sure." I smirked.

"I'll be outside." He grabbed his bag and made his way out the front door, shutting it behind him.

I sighed and looked around my home. The place that would ultimately be where my death takes place. A home was meant to make you feel safe but mine never had. It was where my parents died and it was going to be where I died. Maybe it was never really my home, maybe I didn't have one. My eyes welled up but I refused to let my tears fall. I rubbed my eyes then took in a big breath and made my way to my closet. I grabbed a bag from the hanger and started packing essentials then made my way outside.

"Are you ready to get out of here?" Fenris asked.

I took a deep breath and slowly shrugged my shoulders. "As ready as I'll ever be. Where are we going?" I realised I had never asked him.

"Hunterville," he answered.

CHAPTER 17

MARELLA

The further we walked through the Aldar Forest between Hayselwood and Hunterville, the denser it became. The sweat dripped from my forehead and ran down my cheeks as it became hotter the more we moved. Even though we were in the cooler months, the thick forest and constant walking made it unbearably muggy.

The humidity was definitely taking its toll on me. If we didn't take a break soon I felt like I might just collapse in a heap. To be fair to myself, I had never walked this much since I was mostly secluded to our cottage and Hayselwood.

Fenris was ahead of me by a couple of paces and was clearly more aware of his surroundings than I was. He picked up on every movement and sound, he would stop and gesture for me to do the same whenever he heard something that could potentially be dangerous. Thankfully nothing had bothered us so far. We did see a couple of rabbits run across in front of us, but that was it.

Fenris stopped and took a seat on a tree trunk that had fallen over. "Let's rest for a bit and eat something. It'll be nightfall in a couple of hours and I want to make a dent in our journey before we set up camp." He gestured for me to sit next to him. My feet were so relieved to get some much needed rest.

I opened my bag and grabbed out some water and a sandwich I had prepared earlier. "How long do you think it'll take us to get to Hunterville?" I had never been there before so I had no clue.

"Not too long, a day or less depending on how quickly we travel." He took a bite of his dried meat.

My doubts started to creep in as I thought more and more about this sword. "What if we're walking into a trap?"

"We aren't."

"How can you be so sure?"

He sighed. "I guess I'm not sure but I'm trying to have faith that it will all work out, that we will find this sword."

"I'm just scared," I huffed.

Before I could say more, Fenris held my chin and pulled my face up so I was looking into his eyes. He was so close I could almost touch his lips with mine. I found myself wanting to, but quickly brushed the thought away. I couldn't believe we had come to this, that I could feel this way about a Witch Hunter.

"I get that, but I'm here to take some of that fear off your shoulders. I will do what I can to keep you safe," he said.

I blushed as he dropped his hand and looked away. The tension was overwhelming. How was it not bothering him too? Or was he just better at hiding it than I was?

We finished our food quickly then packed up and headed out again, much to my feet's displeasure. The thick grass and trees were so close together it was a maze to get through them. Gradually, the trees began to move further apart and it was starting to cool down. I could just make out the sun setting in the distance through the trees.

"Stay here and I'll look around for somewhere we can camp. There is nowhere here where we can sleep," Fenris said as he removed his bag.

I waited for what felt like half an hour, taking a seat on a nearby boulder to rest my aching feet, before Fenris finally emerged from the trees.

"Did you find anywhere?" I asked, handing him his bag.

He pointed to the left. "There is a clearing up ahead we can use to our advantage. I'll take you there then I can start a fire and catch us a rabbit to eat."

"How about I start the fire and you catch the rabbit. I'm not completely useless. Besides, I have fire magic so it's kind of a no brainer," I said as I followed him towards the clearing.

"Fair point," Fenris laughed, and I found my heart pounding at the sound. He had a beautiful laugh, it was big and boisterous.

When we got to the clearing we set up our sleeping sacks and Fenris went to catch and skin a rabbit while I started the fire. I tried not to venture too far away from our campsite, so I didn't get lost. I gathered some sticks and brought them back to the clearing, setting them up and starting a fire with my magic as quickly as snapping my fingers.

By the time Fenris got back the moon and stars were above us. He held the skinned rabbit in his hands and got to work cooking it over the fire. When he was done, he handed me some and took a seat next to me.

I chewed off a nice, succulent bit as Fenris did the same. The juice was running down his mouth and I found myself looking at his lips again. I quickly looked away and hoped he didn't notice.

"So, has Hulda always been in your life?" he asked suddenly.

I was thankful for the conversation so I could forget about how my heart raced whenever I gazed at him, or when he was close by.

"Hulda came into my life when I was very young so I don't really remember a time without her," I answered, taking another bite of my rabbit meat.

"You two seem close."

"We are. She's basically raised me since I was six years old."

I hadn't really spoken to anyone about this before so it was a little hard to dredge up the past. I always tried to run from it and shove the thoughts aside. It brought up too many painful memories.

"You don't have to answer… but, what happened with your parents?" He brushed his fingers through his hair and nervously glanced at me.

"Well… Lilith happened. One day the Demon Queen showed up at our cottage and all hell broke loose. The runes around our cottage warned my mother and father. They were able to hide Hulda and I in the crawl space under the cottage. My parents sacrificed their lives to save us. The last thing my mother said was for Hulda to take care of me." My eyes started to well up and I quickly wiped them before any tears could fall. "We still don't know how they got through the wards or why Lilith came and killed my parents. I'm not sure if I ever will know."

Fenris threw the bones of his finished rabbit and took my

hand in his. "I'm sorry you lost your parents so young."

"What about your parents?" I asked, trying to change the subject from me.

He let out a sigh. "I don't know who my parents are. All I know is they are from Valdori and they died when I was born. King Aldric was there when it happened and took me to his kingdom for safety. He's raised me ever since so I guess we have that in common."

"Why hasn't the King told you who your parents are?"

"I brought them up a couple of times when I was younger but he would just tell me he had no idea who they were. That he'd heard screaming coming from an abandoned home then heard a baby cry. When he finally got to my home he found my parents dead on the ground and saw me on the ground near my mother. He said he felt compelled to save me."

He didn't appear to be too bothered by the situation, more accepting of it. Perhaps being so small when it had happened had helped him to move on.

"I'm sorry about your parents, Fenris. That must have been hard to hear."

"I'm sorry for yours too," he answered.

"So... you were raised by the King? That's interesting. How was life growing up in a castle?" I decided to try and steer the conversation to something that may be a bit more cheerful.

"King Aldric has always been good to me, so it has always felt like I was his son. I got to grow up with Princess Lyra who is like a sister to me. Then there's Logan who has lived in the castle his whole life too. His parent's worked for the King so he got to grow up there with me. He wanted to become a Witch Hunter, like me, so the King made it happen."

"Now he's the leader of them." I found myself wanting to

keep him talking, wanting to listen to the deep cadence of his voice... wanting to know all about him. "How did that happen? He's so young, there must be older, more experienced Witch Hunters."

"He's actually the youngest leader we've had. He showed such promise and determination that the King made it happen. Logan is trustworthy and loyal. He's been good for us."

"I'm not going to lie, he does seem tightly wound. But if you say he's been good for the Witch Hunters, then I believe you."

"That's just how Logan is. He's always been a fiery, passionate type of person. Once you get underneath that shield of his he's actually a decent person."

"Well, I'm not sure he will ever like me. We definitely got off on the wrong foot. And not to mention... you know... me being a witch and all."

"Give him time. He'll come around. Especially because of what I told him."

My eyes widened at that. "What did you tell him?"

"I ... ah ... because he knows that there is something between us." He stumbled over his words.

"Oh yeah? What's between us?" I smirked.

"I don't know yet. But I know there is something. I hope you feel it too."

It was then I realised we were still holding hands. "I do."

His cheeks started going red and he cleared his throat. "So, are you ready for this adventure?"

"I'm nervous but I am also excited." I brushed my hair behind my ears. "Fen, I want to thank you again for helping me." I smiled.

"Always." He smiled back.

"So, onto a lighter subject. If you weren't a Witch Hunter

what do you think you'd be doing right now?" I cracked my knuckles.

"Nobody has ever asked me that before and to be honest I'm not quite sure. Being a Witch Hunter is all I've ever known and aspired to be."

"But you don't want to be a Witch Hunter, do you?"

He started fiddling with his bag strap. "I don't think it's my calling. I don't feel comfortable in the role, I never have."

"You should leave then. Do something else, find your calling."

"It's not that easy, unfortunately. I have people who rely on me. The King and Logan."

"If they love you they'll understand."

"Maybe. I don't know." He seemed conflicted.

"Well, I'll be right behind you with whatever you decide." I smiled and Fenris' gaze fell to my lips.

I parted them slightly and his finger came up to brush against them, sending a shiver straight down my spine. He moved closer and pressed a soft kiss against my lips, my heart fluttering at the sensation. He pulled away but gazed into my eyes. He seemed to catch himself, realising what he had done.

"I think maybe we should get some rest." He cleared his throat as he looked away, his cheeks flushed for the umpteenth time tonight. I nodded because words were failing me. He got to his feet and moved away.

Rustling of the trees made me look to the right where I noticed a shadow moving around.

"Did you see that?" I whispered.

Fenris gazed around at where I was looking. "I can't see anything."

"I could have sworn I saw someone."

He walked over to the trees, moving around them and checking thoroughly before walking back. "There's nothing there, are you sure you saw something?"

I pinched the bridge of my nose. "Maybe the stress is making me see things."

"We've both had a long and exhausting day. Get some rest, we'll talk in the morning. I'll take the first watch."

I laid on the ground and put my pack behind my head, rolling over. As I drifted to sleep my thoughts were consumed by Fenris. The way he looked at me and the way his touch sent fire through me, different to my own fire magic. His muscular, tanned olive skin glistened with sweat throughout our journey. I don't know why all of a sudden all I could think of was him. I mean, now that I thought about it, how could I not feel something? He was incredibly attractive and compassionate.

I began drifting further, the last thing I thought of was his smile.

***

"Make a sound and we kill your friend." Hot, fetid breath blasted the side of my face, cold steel pressed against my neck.

I opened my eyes and I was suddenly being pulled into a sitting position and pressed against someone's chest.

"What's going on?" I asked, groggily.

Adrenaline was starting to flare inside of me but I still felt somewhat disoriented from my sleep. My heart was beginning to thrum in my chest and easing some of that grogginess.

"Fucking Bandits." I heard Fenris' voice and peered over to see him being held against a tree by two males, digging his heels in and trying to pull himself free. They struggled to hold him as he put up a fight.

The men all wore similar white, dirty shirts with brown vests and brown long pants. The one holding me had a long, grey beard that smelt like a combination of cigars and dirt. It brushed against my face as he held me to him and made me feel itchy, my skin crawling with his body pressed against mine. The other two men were clean shaven, one with brown hair and the other with black hair, greys peeking out and showing their age.

"Where are you two heading?" the brown-haired bandit asked.

"That's none of your business," I snapped.

The bandit holding me pressed his face against my hair and sniffed then began to feel up my thigh slowly. "You're a feisty one, aren't you?"

"Don't you fucking touch her!" Fenris screamed as he pulled against the two men holding him again, almost breaking free.

"Or fucking what?" The bandit holding me laughed.

"I'll kill you, that's what." Fenris gritted his teeth.

All three of the men roared with laughter.

I could easily take them all out with my fire magic but I risked hurting Fenris in the process. I could withstand the flames, but there was no way he would walk out unscathed.

The man holding me tightened his grip and I yelped in pain. "You'd be wise to answer our questions."

"Leave her alone!" Fenris tried to move towards me but he was being held against that tree so tightly he couldn't, his energy from fighting against them earlier had appeared to run out.

"I'm getting sick of this one." The black haired bandit yanked Fenris back. "Let's just take these weapons and kill them or sell them."

"No. Stick them in the wagon. We can take them with us to Hunterville," the one holding me said.

Well, at least we were heading that way anyway.

The brown haired bandit smirked and before I could reply I watched as they hit Fenris hard on the side of the head with the butt of a pistol. I gasped, feeling the pain as they did the same to me, darkness surrounding my vision until there was nothing.

CHAPTER 18

FENRIS

There was a searing pain in my head. As I tried to open my eyes the light hurt them. I closed them again quickly. The last thing I remembered was seeing Ella being held by that bandit. Seeing her so vulnerable and his disgusting hands on her had me in a fit of rage. I had this strong urge to protect her and keep her safe. Why didn't she use her fire? Was she alright or had they hurt her too?

I finally forced my eyes open and peered around. Sunlight glinted through the trees. Many hours must have passed while we were unconscious. We were just on the outskirts of Hunterville. The buildings of the town were in view up ahead. We were just on the edge of the Aldar Forest, where the path was that entered the town. Why were they here and why did they take us here?

"She's awake," I heard one of the men say.

The man with black hair and horrible breath, as I had learnt earlier when he was so close to my face, came over to where I was trying to get up.

He put his hand on my shoulder and pushed me back down. "Easy there, pal. You took quite a hit."

"No thanks to you," I snarled.

I spotted Ella to my right. She was sitting up against a tree and glaring at the man that held a knife to her throat the night before. The hair on the left of her head was soaked in her blood. I was going to kill these idiots for hurting her. The men walked away and started talking amongst themselves in low voices so we couldn't hear. Ella shuffled closer to me as quietly as she could.

"Be ready, I'll use my fire," Ella whispered so the others wouldn't hear.

"What did you just say?" One of the bandits moved so quickly towards Ella, grabbing her by the chin and wrenching her face up to look at him.

"Stop!" I yelled.

"Oh, we got a lover boy here." The man laughed, and his two friends laughed with him.

Ella grabbed him by the wrist, and he started screaming as her flames ripped into his flesh. He tried to pull away, but she held firm. The other two men rushed at her, shouting "she's a witch!" and cursing. As one of them passed me I used my leg to swipe under his. He fell to the ground heavily as I got to my feet and kicked him in the stomach. He cried out in pain, a crunching sound coming from his ribs upon contact.

Ella summoned her fire, three great big balls of the orange, hot flames hovered above her head. She sent them flying towards the bandits. I ran over to stand by her side. I figured closer to her would be safer than closer to them.

The high-pitched screams and smell of burning flesh hit me as the bandits collapsed, writhing as the flames engulfed them. I moved Ella's face to the side so I could inspect her head. She swayed on her feet.

"Will you be okay?" I asked, holding her upright.

"I just need a moment to regain my strength then I can heal us both. Luckily, they're only small wounds." She pinched the bridge of her nose. "I have the worst headache though."

"You're not alone. Do you think you can make it to the town? We can get a room and rest before we go see the fortune teller?" I still held her arm, afraid she would pass out.

"Yeah, I think I can. Let's find our belongings." She glanced around at the bags until she spotted ours and tried to grab them. I took them from her immediately, there was no way I was letting her carry them in this state.

"We may as well look in their wagon and see if there is anything useful," I said, and she nodded.

They had bags and chests heaped together within the wagon. We rifled through them, Ella going at an easy pace. We managed to find some pistols, three bags full of coins and several maps. We left the pistols since I had runed ones anyway, then shoved the rest of the items in our bags. Ella then set the rest on fire. She was able to contain any flames she made so they wouldn't burn down the trees.

My feet were aching, my head was pounding, and I felt like I could sleep for days. Ella appeared far worse than I did. I was grateful those idiots had at least stopped close to town. We started moving slowly towards Hunterville, holding onto each other for support because of our injuries. I struggled under the weight of the packs, but Ella could barely hold herself up so I gritted my teeth and kept going.

The town was smaller than Hayselwood, with a tiny main street, thatched cottages, and it didn't contain as many people or shops. The tavern was off to the side and there was no church. Witch Hunters within Hayselwood were expected to service Hunterville on a rotating monthly roster. Logan and I were never on that roster as the King preferred us in Hayselwood where the church was.

As we approached the town I looked around and saw an Inn not too far away. "We can go there," I said, pointing to the building. Ella was still in my grasp, her face was sickly pale. I pulled her up to support her more and ignored my own pain. "Ella, are you okay?"

"I think I'm going to be sick," she whispered.

Her body suddenly went limp in my arms and I had to use what little energy I had left to prevent myself from falling to the ground. The weight of the packs and an unconscious Ella almost brought me down.

I hurriedly pulled her towards the inn entrance, half dragging and half carrying her weight. "Somebody help me," I yelled frantically.

An older woman moved away from the bar and rushed over to us. "What's happened?" she asked.

"My friend and I were attacked by bandits. We were both hit on the head," I replied, moving further into the inn.

"Gerard, we need assistance over here," the woman called out.

It was then I realised the whole place had gone quiet and everyone was staring at us. I didn't care though, all I cared about was making sure Ella was alright.

A bigger man with a long grey beard and muscled, large arms came over and gently picked Ella up. "Follow me. I'll take you to a room," Gerard said.

We rushed up some stairs, the woman taking our bags off my shoulders and allowing me to lean against her since I was weak myself. She stopped in front of a door and burst into the room where Gerard placed Ella on a bed then left.

The woman moved Ella's head to the side where it was wet with her blood, the wound was still bleeding profusely which wasn't a good sign. I was thankful that I was the only person in the room able to smell the earthy scent of her witch blood. My necklace, provided by the Witch Hunters, allowed this ability. I didn't think this woman would be the kind of person to turn Ella in, but I sure wasn't going to take any risks. I watched her carefully through blurry eyes though, just in case.

Gerard returned moments later with a bowl of clean water and some fabric. I fell into a chair, my exhaustion finally taking over. I fought to stay awake, not willing to take my eyes off Ella for even a moment. The woman cleaned Ella's wound gently, placing the fabric in the water, ringing it out then dabbing it gently over the wound. When she was done Gerard took the now dirty bowl away and she came to stand next to where I was sitting.

"She will be fine, the wound isn't deep and it has stopped bleeding now. She just needs to rest." She handed me a vial from her pockets. "This is a tonic that will help the pain somewhat. I have several on hand. The amount of people who find themselves in my inn because of an injury they procured somewhere. If I had a coin for every time ... well, I'd probably have several inns by now." She shook her head.

"Thank you for your hospitality. What's your name?" I

asked.

"My name is Mable and I will always help a Witch Hunter. You do keep us safe after all." She squeezed my shoulder.

I bit my lip. "I don't suppose I could trouble you for some water?"

"I'll have Gerard bring you up some water and food. How are you feeling? You don't seem well yourself," she noted.

"I think I'll be fine. Other than a pounding headache I feel okay. I just want to make sure Ella is alright."

"That's Ella I presume. What is your name then?"

"I'm Fenris."

"Oh, I've heard of you. You're one of the top Witch Hunters. You live in the castle don't you?"

"I live in both the castle and the church," I answered cautiously.

She must have sensed my suspicion. "I'm of no threat to you, I've just heard stories. It's nice to finally meet you. If you need anything at all please let us know." She turned and walked out the door, leaving me alone with Ella.

The room was small and musty, but it was enough for the one night we needed it for. The bed Ella was laying in was big with enough room for two people to sleep on and there was a long red fabric couch opposite it. The carpets were an ugly grey colour and there was a large window with thick dark blue curtains. The bathroom door was beside the couch and contained a bath and sink. Two white towels hung from a broken towel rack next to the sink. It was modest, but it was all we needed.

I moved towards the bed where Ella was still sleeping. Pulling the blanket from under her legs and placing it over her, she stirred and rolled over but remained asleep, hair falling over her face. I brushed it gently behind her ear. She was so incredibly beautiful. It was hard to tear my eyes away from her.

I sat there for a moment longer before getting to my feet and heading to the bathroom. I had to get the mud and blood off my body, it was caked on, making me feel uncomfortable and dirty.

After I finished I wrapped the towel around my hips and moved back into the bedroom to find Ella sitting up on the bed, very much awake but disorientated. I suddenly felt vulnerable that I was only in a towel. She peered up at me and her lips parted. Those beautiful lips that I could not stop thinking about.

It was at that moment Mable came barging through the door with Gerard close behind her carrying bowls and cups of water. The smell filled the room and my stomach growled. I was annoyed they had chosen this moment to come in, thoughts filling my head of what could have happened.

"I have some vegetable stew and water for you both," Mable said as Gerard placed it on the table in the corner. Mable pointedly ignored me in my towel. I'm sure she'd seen worse. "Oh, Ella dear, you're awake. That's wonderful."

"Wait... what's going on? Who are you?" Ella asked.

"My name is Mable and I own this establishment that you're currently staying at. I also cleaned your nasty wound. You'll be fine, just take it easy."

"Thank you, Mable," Ella said.

Mable shrugged. "It's what I do, dear."

I walked over to Mable and placed a bag of coins in her hand that I had fished from my bag.

Her eyes went wide. "Bandits didn't get your coin, I see." She grabbed the bag and put it in her pocket.

"They didn't get anything." I smirked.

"Excellent. I'm glad," she said.

They both walked out the door, leaving Ella and I to ourselves. I was so hungry I didn't even bother to dress.

The vegetable stew smelt incredible and tasted just as good. It was soothing and just what we needed after what happened. We ate our meals and drank our water in silence. We were both completely exhausted.

"I might go wash up now," Ella said, gesturing to the bathroom.

I felt nervous, being in a bedroom with her alone. I knew I wanted her, craved her even. "Before you go, Mable gave me this tonic to give to you." I handed the vial to her.

"Ah, a pain tonic. That was really nice of her." Ella took the top off and drank the entire bottle.

"How did you know it was a pain tonic?" I asked, surprised.

"When you grow up around a healer you pick up a thing or two." She placed the vial on the table then walked into the bathroom and closed the door.

All I could think about was the soapy water all over her perfect body, washing her breasts and the rest of her. I went to readjust myself only to realise I was still only in my towel. Not wanting to tempt fate, I got up and dressed then sat on the couch waiting for her to finish up.

When she emerged from the bathroom my breath caught in my throat. Her hair was wet and her cheeks rosy red. She was alluring. Part of me wanted to grab her and throw her on the bed. I gulped at the thought, shoving it down.

"I'll take the couch and you can take the bed." I got up and grabbed a pillow from the bed, taking it back to the couch.

"Are you sure? That couch looks pretty uncomfortable."

I put the pillow behind my head and laid down. "It's so comfortable," I laughed, and Ella laughed as well. "I'll be fine. It's just for one night."

She didn't look convinced. To prove a point, she sauntered over, laying right next to me on the couch. She scooched right up close to me, her warm soft body nestling into my side, and her face barely centimetres from mine. Her sweet smell washed over me, my manhood betraying me again. I hoped she didn't notice.

"Hmm, you're right. This is *so* comfortable," she teased.

We burst into a fit of laughter. She hopped up and made her way to the bed, sliding in. She draped the covers over herself and moved so she was on her side. I was disappointed and missed her warmth, but I couldn't muster the courage to say or do anything.

As I rested my head on the pillow I started to think about everything I had learnt so far about witches. It got me wondering and I immediately panicked when a thought popped into my head.

"Before you go to sleep can I ask you a question?" I sat up on the couch.

"Okay, I'm listening," she replied.

"Can witches read minds?" I was worried if she could read minds then she'd know all my most recent thoughts about her.

She chuckled. "No, we can't read minds. Your secrets are safe."

I let out a breath, thankful that my thoughts were still my own. Ella made me feel happy which was something I realised I never experienced in its true capacity.

Thinking about my duty as a Witch Hunter, the fact I was trained to take down witches, made me want to give it up for good. I knew after all of this I could never hurt a witch or even watch as other Witch Hunters hurt witches. It wasn't something that called to me anymore, I don't think it ever did. The only good thing to come from Witch Hunters was the eradication of demons.

I heard rustling and looked over to see Ella sit up in the bed.

"What is it?" I asked.

She furrowed her eyebrows. "It should feel wrong, Fen, to confide in you about things that witches have kept secret for so long. Especially because of your... profession. But I don't. I feel the opposite. Something inside of me keeps telling me to trust you. That's why I took you to my home, and it's why I agreed to come with you to find this sword."

"You can trust me, Ella. I would never do anything to hurt you. In fact, I..." I trailed off.

Ella sighed. "Well, if we've established that I trust you, and you trust me, there's no reason for you to be sleeping on that couch that I know is uncomfortable."

I was about to protest but she started talking again before I could get a word in. "Fen, we both got attacked by bandits and barely made it out with our lives. You had to carry me here. We both deserve a good night's sleep."

The couch did feel lumpy and hard against my back so I got up and moved towards the bed. In truth, she didn't have to convince me very much at all. She threw the blanket out so I could climb in.

"Are you tired?" she asked.

We both faced each other with our heads against the pillow.

"Yes... and no." I wanted to keep talking to her, getting to know her.

"Tell me a secret then... something about you that nobody

else knows."

"That's going to be hard. Logan knows everything about me."

"Just... think."

I paused for a moment, trying to conjure something up from my memories and thoughts. "I think... I don't want to do it anymore..." I met her eyes. "Be a Witch Hunter, that is." Saying it out loud felt... odd.

Ella moved closer to me and she laced her fingers between mine under the blanket. "I don't think it's the path for you. I feel like... I truly believe you're destined for greater things, Fen."

"I think you are too, Ella."

She looked away. "Did you forget how slim my chance is of making any destiny for myself, great or small?"

"No. I haven't forgotten. But that's why we're on this journey. So that you have a long, fantastic life ahead of you, filled with great deeds."

She gazed into my eyes. "I want to forget. Just for tonight. Help me forget, Fen?"

"How?" I furrowed my eyebrows, not entirely sure what she was suggesting. I didn't want to get my hopes up.

"Like this." She planted her lips on mine.

I never realised how hungry I was for her until I tasted the saltiness of her lips. I slid one of my arms underneath her head and grabbed her waist with the other as my tongue met hers. My heart thundered in my chest, my need for her trailing all the way down to the bulge in my pants.

She pulled away panting. "Is this alright?"

"Does that feel like it's alright to you, Ella?" I smirked as I rocked my bulge against her and her eyes widened as she grinned.

Our lips met again as I slid my hand slowly up her shirt, finding her breasts bare, she gasped as I grazed her nipple. I broke the kiss so I could pull her shirt over her head and I ripped my own off, desperate for more of her mouth. My lips moved upon hers again as I slid my hand from her breast around to the middle of her back, moving down and tucking my fingers under the waist of her pants. I pulled away from her, panting.

"May I?" I whispered against her lips.

"Please!" she said, all breathy.

I tugged her pants and underwear down gently but quickly as my desire for her was searing through me. I groaned as Ella trailed her fingers down my stomach and palmed my bulge through my pants.

I couldn't take it any longer, I had to touch more of her, explore her body. I moved my hand up her thigh, feeling her shudder beneath my touch. I pulled her leg closer towards me so her legs were further apart, her centre bare, while I trailed kisses against her neck. I looked up, her eyes were closed and her lips parted.

"How does this feel?" I asked as my teeth grazed her nipple.

She groaned in response and moved her head to the side.

"What about this?" I asked as I softly trailed my fingers up and down the slickness between her legs.

"More, please!" she begged, arching her back and making me want to taste more of her breasts.

I tenderly kissed around her nipples as I stroked her centre with my fingers. Gathering her slickness and swirling it around. She moved her legs apart further as I continued to pleasure her. I flicked and rubbed and circled her sensitive nub, pushing her closer to her release. She rolled her hips under me, trying to create more friction. She spread her legs further again and arched her back, suddenly crying out from her orgasm.

I climbed on top of her carefully and brushed her hair with my fingers, using the opposite hand from the one I used to pleasure her with. "How are you feeling?"

"Happy." She pulled me down and kissed me.

I cupped her breast as my bulge pressed against her stomach.

She grasped me, feeling the length of me, moving her hand up and down. I threw my head back and closed my eyes, savouring her touch.

"Will you?" she asked, moving her hand to feel around my back.

She didn't have to complete that sentence, I knew exactly what she wanted. "Have you done this before?" I asked.

"No... I... there has never been anyone to do it with," she answered, looking down.

I pulled her face back up with her chin and gazed into her eyes. "You don't have to be frightened. I will never hurt you or judge you, Ella."

She smiled and gently kissed my lips. "Thank you."

"Do you take the birth control tonic?" I asked, wanting to make sure we were both playing it safe.

"Yes, I take it every month to help with my bleeding," she said and I nodded.

"This will hurt at first. Tell me if you want to stop."

She nodded in response.

I positioned myself over her entrance and felt the wetness that had accumulated from her previous orgasm. I slipped into her slowly, inch by inch, allowing her to accommodate to me, not willing to hurt her any more than I already knew I would. She flinched slightly, and I slowed, but she pulled my hips toward her, encouraging me to keep going. With one final, slow stroke, I was fully inside of her.

"Are you okay?" I asked.

"Yes. Keep going." She was breathless.

I rocked back and forth, her legs opening wider for me as the pleasure started to take over the pain. I trailed my hand down her collarbone and over her breast, cupping it with my hand and massaging. She groaned and started to move with me.

I moved faster and more desperately, as if I couldn't get enough of her until finally I exploded.

With us both panting, I carefully moved out of her and fell to the side, laying down.

"Woah," she whispered through her breaths.

"I didn't hurt you too much did I?"

"It was a bit uncomfortable at first but you more than made up for it." She turned over to me and kissed my nose, snuggling into my chest.

I wrapped my arms around her and kissed the top of her head, breathing in the sweet jasmine scent of her hair. I was more happy in this moment than I had ever been before and I was grateful I had found her.

"I could kiss Andras right now!" I said.

Ella peered up at me with raised eyebrows. "Ahh... why?"

I kissed her forehead. "If he hadn't tried to kill you that night, and I hadn't stepped in to save you ... I might have missed out on this."

Ella stretched up and kissed me. "Thanks be to Andras, then," she murmured against my lips.

I squeezed her arm. "I'll be right back."

"Where are you going?" she asked as I got off the bed.

I didn't answer, I walked into the bathroom and grabbed a

cloth, wetting it with warm water then taking it to her.

"What's that for?" She glanced down at the cloth.

"For me to clean my mess." I pointed between her legs.

"You don't have to do that."

"I want to."

She smiled and nodded. I took my time cleaning her, mesmerised by her beautiful body. She was so utterly perfect to me and I eventually had to stop or I feared I'd want to go again.

"I'm going to go run you a bath then I think we should take full advantage of this bed and get some rest." I kissed her forehead then slipped out of the bed, I was still completely naked and felt the cool air of the night against my skin. I felt her eyes on me as I walked away, making me feel warm inside.

I filled up the bath with steamy water then went back into the bedroom. Ella glanced up at me and smiled.

"You're beautiful... your smile, your body, the way you carry yourself. Every part of you is beautiful."

She blushed. "You keep talking like that and I'll find myself too big for my boots."

"Good." I put one arm under her head and the other under her legs then scooped her up, carrying her to the bathroom.

I lowered her slowly into the bath and she groaned. "This water is wonderful."

I picked up a sponge and began rubbing soap into her shoulders and down over her breasts.

"If you keep doing that I may not be able to hold back from round two, but I think I may be a bit sore for that just yet." She smirked.

I dropped the sponge into the bath and leant down to kiss her head. "Come on, let's get you to bed. To sleep. Because we are going to get that sword, and there will be all of the time in the world for round two, and three, and twenty." The thought of that made me happy.

Ella was silent and stared down at her fingers as she twirled them in the water. I could tell it was getting to her, the reminders of the vision.

I grabbed her hand to stop her from fidgeting and helped her to her feet, grabbing a towel from the rack and wrapping it around her.

She climbed out of the bath and I silently dried her off then threw the towel on the ground. We walked out of the bathroom hand in hand, I watched her naked body return to the bed, admiring every inch of her. I didn't bother with clothes either, wrapping my own naked body around her and pulling her back to rest her head on my bare chest.

She smiled and furrowed her eyebrows as she gazed up into my eyes. "Thank you. For always caring and just being here for me."

"I will never abandon you, Ella."

I kissed her softly against her lips as I squeezed her shoulder close. She was warm and comforting and it all felt right.

But my chest began to hurt as I wondered was this the start of something that may never be?

CHAPTER 19

MARELLA

When I woke up still nestled into Fenris' chest. It was warm and comforting and I never wanted to leave. It was my new favourite place to be.

I felt him stir then rub my arm. "How are you feeling?"

Although I didn't want to move I knew we had to so I sat up and looked down at him. "My head is throbbing again. I think I should have enough energy to heal our wounds now. We are very lucky it wasn't worse than this."

"I agree. We have got to be more careful from now on," he said.

"Can you help me with mine?" I asked, moving towards the end of the bed.

It was then I realised we were both still very naked. Somehow I didn't care, I felt more comfortable with Fenris than I'd ever felt with anyone.

He crawled towards me and sat behind me. "What did you need me to do?"

I had to pull my gaze away from his muscular body, the chest hairs sending me wild. "If you could place my hand on my wound I should be able to heal it," I said.

He trailed his fingers down my arm creating instantaneous goosebumps then grabbed my hand, lifting it up to my head and gently onto my wound.

I hissed in pain but felt relief the second my magic flowed into the wound. It was as if my energy was flowing out of me then back into where it was needed most. I felt my magic cut off, letting me know the healing was complete. I felt no pain in my head anymore and smiled with relief.

Fenris was staring at my breasts, a smile upon his lips. "You're so beautiful, Ella."

I grabbed him around the back of his neck and brought him down against my mouth, taking in as much of him as I could get. We pulled away and I was instantly saddened by the loss of his lips touching mine.

"You need to be careful, Fen. We don't have time for this but I honestly can't help myself with you." I smirked.

"Neither can I." He looked into my eyes before placing a gentle kiss against my cheek.

I cleared my throat. "Alright, it's your turn. Sit on the end of the bed," I ordered.

"Are you sure you have enough energy to heal us both?" Fenris sat on the bed, uncertainty in his tone.

"They are only small wounds, I'll be fine."

I placed my hand over his head and began working on healing him. The wound was much smaller than mine, requiring less time to heal. When it was all done we reluctantly got dressed, grabbed our belongings and headed down the stairs. Mable was behind the bar and when she saw us, she waved.

"I hope you both had a good night. Where are you heading to now?" she asked as I handed her the room key.

"Have you ever heard of a fortune teller named Marge that resides here?" I was hopeful she could point us in the right direction.

"What could you possibly want that horrid woman for?" Mable replied.

"Wait, you don't like her?" I asked.

"She's rude and the prices for her knowledge are always too high. It's ridiculous."

"In any case, she has something we need," Fenris answered.

"Whatever you need from that woman is not worth the price, trust me. Nobody has ever made a good deal with her." Mable answered. She grabbed a cloth and started moving around wiping down tables.

I wandered behind her. "We need to speak with her. It is life or death. Whatever she wants she can have."

Mable sighed and stopped wiping down the table. She looked up at me. "Just don't say I didn't warn you." She pointed towards the door. "As you head outside, turn right and start walking. You'll come across her shop after a couple of minutes. She has a big sign, so you won't miss it."

"Thank you. We appreciate everything." I nodded at Mable, and she nodded back.

Fenris and I headed out and began walking towards where Mable said to go. We walked past several shops and market stalls, the merchants trying to sell us their latest items. One of them, an older man, tried to put something in my hands and I had to shove the items away. They all seemed pushier here than in Hayselwood. It made me realise our town was more vibrant, and friendlier. The people here seemed almost desperate.

There were several people standing around, their clothes tattered and their bodies frail. Why would Hunterville be worse off than us? We were neighbouring towns. They weren't that much smaller than Hayselwood. If I survived, I vowed to look into it. To see if there was anything I could do to help.

Mable was right, it only took a couple of minutes before we were standing out the front of the fortune teller's shop. The sign read 'Marge's Fortunes' in white and was surrounded by a purple background. The shop windows were closed with black curtains.

I hesitantly opened the door and as Fenris and I walked in, it closed by itself. The room was dark and mostly empty. There were a couple of trinkets here and there and a counter, but nobody was behind it. A black curtain was half open behind the counter which showed the back room. I could see a table with a purple tablecloth and two chairs either side of it. On top of the table there was a crystal ball.

"What do you want?" A raspy voice broke the silence.

An older woman with liver spotted skin and sparse, white hair that stuck out in all directions, opened the black curtain completely and walked out.

"Are you Marge?" Fenris asked, stepping closer so he was right beside me. We were so close, it was like a spark was buzzing between us.

"Who wants to know?" she snapped, crossing her wrinkled arms against her chest.

"I'm Ella and this is Fenris. I'll just get straight to the point.

Someone we know told us you could help us find an item."

"And what item might that be?" She uncrossed her arms, placing them on her hips. Mable was right, she was horrid.

"The Sword of Fatum," Fenris answered.

Marge's eyes went wide as she took a seat on a chair behind the counter. "What could you possibly need with that?"

"Aren't you supposed to be a fortune teller? Shouldn't you know why we're here?" I was starting to lose my patience.

"It doesn't work like that, girl."

"Look, we've come a long way. What do we have to do to get this information?" I asked and Fenris added. "Mable said you have a price?"

Marge huffed. "Answer my question and I might consider helping you."

"We need it to save someone's life against Lilith," Fenris said, moving slightly in front of me.

"Ah, the Demon Queen. What makes you think you can go up against her?" Marge tapped her fingers against the counter.

"We don't have a choice," I choked out.

Marge grinned. "Ah, so it's your life that needs saving then?"

I rubbed my arms. "Please just help us, we will give you anything, do anything," I pleaded.

I didn't realise how much I truly wanted to live until this moment. Until all was riding on us finding this sword and this fortune teller had the answer, but was being difficult.

"Be careful what you say, girl. You may regret what you give up."

"If I die then what's the point anyway?" I threw my arms up in the air, frustration seeping in.

Marge tapped her finger against her chin. "I'll tell you what... I'll tell you where the sword is in exchange for something."

Marge smiled and as she did, I could see her dirty, yellowing teeth.

"So, you don't have the sword here?" Fenris posed a good question.

"No, I do not. But I know exactly where it is."

"What do you want in return?" I narrowed my eyes, knowing she was about to ask for something ridiculous, just like Mable said.

"I'll take your first born child." Marge smirked.

"You can't be serious?" I scoffed.

"Why not? You get the sword and I get your first born child. That seems fair to me." Marge chuckled.

"Wait... whose first born child? Mine or hers?" Fenris asked.

"What makes you think you won't have a child together?" Marge raised her eyebrows.

Fenris turned to me. "Ella, if we don't get that sword there won't be a first born."

My mouth fell open. "Are you seriously considering this?"

His eyes fell to the ground. "I don't know how else to save your life."

"No way. We'll find it on our own thank you." I couldn't believe the audacity of her. To even ask such a thing.

Fenris looked conflicted but he nodded and we began to leave but stopped when we heard her laughing. "Oh, come back here I was only kidding. What could I do with a baby anyway? Annoying little things. No, what I want in return for the location of the sword is something simple. Your blood." She pointed at Fenris.

"What could you possibly want with his blood?" I asked, confused.

"That's none of your business. Do we have a deal or not?

You're wasting my time now."

Fenris relented. "Fine. I'll give you my blood."

"Fenris, you don't have to do that. We can find another way," I whispered.

"There is no other way, Ella. We don't know how much time you have left. Besides, what could she do with it anyway?" Fenris took the knife and vial Marge held out to him and cut his finger.

I watched as his red blood pooled into the vial like a thick wine. He handed it back and she smiled.

"Here's a map to the location. Safe travels." She handed us the map.

"Wait a second. Did you have that with you the whole time?" I asked.

Fenris took out a bandage from his pack and wrapped his hand with it. "You knew we were coming. You knew what we wanted, didn't you?" he questioned her.

Marge chuckled. "You both best be on your way now." She ignored Fenris' questions.

As we turned to walk out the door I heard her croaky voice behind us. "Oh, and just so you know, Lilith is destined to take over and destroy the world. Good luck." Marge cackled and walked out the back with the vial of Fenris' blood, completely closing the black curtain.

CHAPTER 20

FENRIS

W e sat at the bar in Mable's Inn, going over the map together to figure out our next steps.

"Okay, so it looks like we head north-west into the Crostwell Forest," I said, pointing at a spot on the map.

"Wait, I know that name. There's something in that forest. Hulda told me about it years ago. She said to keep my distance." Ella's eyes moved around the map.

"Do you remember why?" I asked, looking up at her.

She furrowed her eyebrows. "I think a coven of witches lives there. We need to be careful."

"Why should we be concerned? I thought witches took care of their own?" I rested my cheek against my fist, my elbow leaning on the table.

"Not all witches are good just like not all humans are good.

We wouldn't go wandering into a home we don't know. We have to be on our guard. I don't know what they're like and I don't know them." Ella brushed her hands over her face.

"Are you okay?" I asked, placing my hand on her shoulder.

"I think this is just all getting to me. The stress and the fact that all of this is necessary at all. My fate is putting you in constant danger, and that doesn't feel right to me."

"Hey, I chose to come. We can get through this. We just have to get the sword and get home. Easy enough." I gave her a smile.

"I'm glad one of us can make light of this situation." Ella teasingly shoved me.

"I guess all we've done so far is sleep rough, escape a gang of bandits, and seriously consider giving the soul of our first born to a crazy fortune teller ... it's just an average day for us, really!" I said, sarcastically.

"Did you really believe what she said about that?" she asked.

"You heard her. Besides, when we get that sword and move past all of this, I want a first born, a second born and maybe even a fifth born... with you."

Ella blushed and pushed her hair behind her ears. "Let's not get too far ahead of ourselves. You're not the one who has to give birth to them." She smiled and picked up the map. I enjoyed the way her eyes lit up when she smiled.

"There's no such thing as too far ahead with you." I leant down and kissed her forehead. "I guess we better get going. Try and get some distance before the sun goes down." I got to my feet and held my hand out. Ella took to the gesture, pulling herself up.

She packed the map into her bag and slung it over her shoulder, then we headed out the door with the sun still blaring down on us. It was hard to believe just yesterday we were on the brink of death.

Walking to the edge of the Crostwell Forest only took about half an hour. As we entered, I felt a cool breeze flowing through the trees, ruffling my hair. It was going to be a nice day so long as we didn't run into any trouble. I was hoping I could get Ella to enjoy it as much as she could considering the situation. The more I spent time with her the more I realised my feelings for her were growing. I didn't quite understand them, and I didn't know what to do about them, but I couldn't deny the way she made me feel. I wanted to spend everyday with her going on adventures and just being in each other's company.

As we walked into the Crostwell Forest, there was an abundance of animals and I couldn't help but stop to appreciate the sight. There were birds whistling in the trees and a rabbit running across the path in front of us. Ella turned to me.

"Why are we stopping? We only just got here," she asked, walking closer.

"Just taking it all in. Don't you love nature? Animals? Being outside?" I closed the rest of the distance between us, and we were so close I could feel her breath on my cheek.

"You're right. It is very beautiful." Ella grabbed my hand and I could feel my heart begin to race.

I brushed some hair behind her ear that had come loose from the wind and pulled her face into mine, crushing our lips together in a fiery kiss. I grabbed her waist and pulled her in closer, deepening the kiss as she placed her arms behind my neck. I got caught up in the moment and lifted her, pushing her against a tree as she wrapped her legs around me, her tongue dancing over mine. She broke the kiss, looking into my eyes, her own sparkling and her chest heaving.

"That was..." I couldn't finish the sentence; I was still trying to catch my breath.

"Perfect," Ella finished.

"You're perfect." I smiled.

Ella grinned, then leaned back, biting her lip. "What is happening here? I mean, between us."

I set her down, my thumbs caressing her waist. "I'm not quite sure, but I'm willing to explore it, if you are."

She looked in thought for a moment. "Let's just see if we make it out the other side of this, before we go making any declarations."

"Hey... we aren't going to let anything happen to you. I will do everything in my power to stop it."

"I know, Fen. I just don't want to give myself too much false hope."

I sighed, the moment getting away from us. "I understand."

"We better get going." I watched her walk away, my stomach tightening. We had to succeed. I was not prepared to lose a chance at a future with her.

Our conversation as the day wore on remained firmly in small-talk. There was no more discussion of that kiss, or her imminent death hanging over us like a pall.

As night fell, a cool breeze sprung up, making Ella shiver. We began searching for somewhere to set up camp. We came upon a small cave-like area moments later which was perfect to shelter for the night and start a fire. I took out some bread from my pack that I'd brought from Mable's Inn and handed some to Ella.

"I didn't even see you grab that!" She smiled and ate some, her eyes closing.

"I guess I'm just too good a thief." I laughed.

"You are the furthest thing from a thief." She pushed against my shoulder, laughing.

I smiled, my chest filling with warmth as I draped my arm around her shoulder and she nestled into me. This is something I could happily get used to.

"I'll go grab some wood and sticks for you to make a fire. It's getting way too cold." I got up off the ground and ventured through the trees, keeping close by.

When I got back Ella had a book in her hands, fire dancing in her palm over the pages. She was concentrating so hard she didn't even notice me until I dropped the pile in front of her, causing her to jump and look up, her flames extinguishing.

"Sorry I startled you. What are you reading?" I asked.

"It's my mother's grimoire," she said, as she wrapped it back in the leather she had on her lap and put it back in her pack. She stood to help me build the fire. "I take it everywhere with me and usually read it every night. It makes me feel close to her."

Ella flicked her wrist and flames immediately emerged within her hand. She knelt down and pushed the ball of fire into the sticks I had gathered and it all went up in flames, lighting the area as though it wasn't even night time. It was something I would never get tired of seeing, her using her magic.

"So, since we have time, let's list off what we know about this sword so far," Ella asked, taking a seat.

"It can change someone's destiny. I think that's all we know about it. That and we now have an idea of the location," I replied, taking a seat next to her.

Ella groaned. "We need to find out more information. I just don't know how."

"Well, Imogen, our head kitchen maid, used to tell Logan and

I stories. I don't remember much but Logan and her reminded me of a couple of things."

"Stories always tend to have a grounding in the truth, so come on, out with it." She waved her hand at me.

I cleared my throat. "The sword was crafted by a demon. His wife was a witch and helped him create it." As I recounted the details Imogen had told me not long ago I started to recall more of the story. It was as if a switch had turned on inside my brain. "The demon died before he could use it. I remember Imogen saying it can only be used once. The sword will turn to ash, disappearing in the wind afterwards."

"But how are we supposed to change my destiny with a sword?" Ella picked up a stick and stoked the fire.

"I'm not sure. But I would say it would require using the sword how it's intended to be used. Stabbing," I winced.

Ella turned her lip up. "That just sounds like I'll die anyway."

"Maybe not. Maybe we can figure out a way to bring you back once it's done, or have Hulda on hand to heal you. But we should find out first before we risk it and... you know... stab you."

"I'm inclined to agree with you." She placed her head in her hands and groaned.

"Are you okay?" I wrapped my arm around her.

"I just feel like we are on this exhausting journey to get a sword that we know barely anything about and we don't even know how we use it once we get it. Maybe we should have stayed back and done more research first."

"We couldn't risk it, Ella. You have no idea how much time you have left. This could be our only shot. And the further away we are from that cottage, the better."

"I know." She got to her feet. "I just wish we knew more."

She walked towards the opening of the cave and leant against the stone entrance.

Her shoulders began to shake as she sniffled, her hands moving up towards her eyes to wipe them. What could I do? What could I say? I had no idea how to make this right and comfort her when we didn't know what the future would hold.

I got to my feet and walked over to her, pulling her into my arms and letting her cry into my chest, not saying a word.

CHAPTER 21

MARELLA

My eyes fluttered open, the brightness from the sun flooding into the cave. Fenris hadn't woken me up to take second watch for the night.

I sat up and looked over to see him leaning against the side of the opening of the cave where we stood just hours ago. Where he held me while I cried. His eyes seemed to be staring off into the distance and he was frowning. I knew what we spoke about last night worried him just as much as it did me. Somehow, we had gotten to a point where this wasn't just a friendly relationship anymore, this was turning into something serious. He meant something to me and I knew I meant something to him.

Fenris looked at me and straightened up. "Are you ready to get going?" He walked towards me.

"As ready as I'll ever be." I half smiled.

"I know it's hard but try not to stress too much. Once we get the sword we will figure the rest out." He held his hand out and I took it, getting to my feet.

I sighed and got my things ready before we both headed out.

We walked in silence for what felt like hours, Fenris stopping to check the map every now and again. He was clearly exhausted, but he hadn't complained at all. We finally made it to the clearing that was marked on the map but nothing was in sight.

"This can't be it. There's nothing here." Fenris spun around.

"There has to be something, surely."

"Unless that fortune teller lied to us."

"Dammit!" The fire inside me rose and danced on my fingertips but I calmed myself down and made them vanish. "That stupid old hag! I can't believe she lied to us!" We couldn't afford the continuous setbacks.

"Let's just look around before we give up." Fenris folded up the map and put it in his pocket before heading over to the trees.

We spent the next two hours running our fingers over trees, looking for knots that might open a hidden compartment, or hollows where a sword might be stashed before finally meeting in the middle of the clearing again.

"Can I accept defeat now?" I asked Fenris.

"This is ridiculous. We have to go back to Marge and confront her. Give her back her useless map." Fenris threw the map to the ground and it landed in a puddle of dirty water.

I picked it up, brushing away some of the muddy water. "Wait, Fen ... look!" I held the map up to his face, where before our eyes the design on it was changing. His mouth fell open in shock.

"It's underground," he answered as a matter of fact. "There's some writing here … 'The blood of one borne of magic, spilled upon the ground. Aperta will reveal where your treasure can be found.' That's interesting."

"Borne of magic. I'm a witch so it has to be me that opens it." I looked up at him to see him frown.

"I really hate the idea of you having to cut yourself," he said.

"Do you want us to get that sword or not?"

He sighed and unsheathed his dagger from his hip, handing it to me. "Fine."

As I took it from him I moved it around in my hand, studying the runes. "These runes won't kill me will they? Since I'm a witch. They won't kill me if I cut myself?" I was suddenly nervous.

"The runes don't work like that." He turned the dagger still in my hand to show the butt. "See this symbol here? That's mine. Which means for the runes to be activated I have to be wielding the weapon."

"Runes seem an awful lot like magic. I don't understand how Witch Hunters can despise us yet use such abilities."

"I guess in a way they kind of are. Runes have been used throughout history with Witch Hunters. If I'm being honest, I'm not quite sure where they came from. The scholars take care of them all, embedding them into our weapons and buildings," Fenris explained.

I paused for a moment. "Buildings?"

"How do you think witches and demons are forbidden from entering the castle or the church?"

My eyes widened. "You have runes all over the buildings. That's… kind of genius."

"I wish it didn't keep everyone out though." Fenris' eyes gazed into mine.

I needed to do something before we decided to take each other on the forest floor, the moment getting way too heated.

I hissed as I slid the blade against the palm of my hand, then I turned my hand palm down and watched the droplets of blood fall to the ground.

"Aperta!" I spoke loudly and confidently, and after a moment the ground began to shake beneath our feet.

We quickly darted out of the way as the ground began to move, shaking and rumbling loudly. When the dust finally cleared from the movement of it all, we saw several stairs that headed into darkness. We couldn't see anything else as they disappeared deep into the ground.

CHAPTER 22

FENRIS

E lla went to walk straight in and I had to grab her arm to pull her back.

"We need to be careful. We are walking into the unknown and there could be anything down there. Let me go first and watch your steps," I whispered in her ear as I held her close. Her body warm against my own, sending shivers down my spine.

"Okay," she replied breathlessly, holding her hands up in surrender.

I took a few steps but was soon swallowed by darkness. We needed light. It was pitch black. Ella must have sensed what I was thinking because flames encased her palm in seconds. She stood by my side with a smirk on her face, her flames lighting the entrance to the cave. The stone stairs descended well beyond the reach of her light. On either side of the stairwell there were small holes in the stone.

"This place is boobytrapped," I hissed, gripping her elbow. "We need to move very carefully."

I looked attentively at each step as I descended and every now and again I saw a stone that was not quite like the others that would surely set off the trap. The stairs went on for what felt like hours, my legs burning with the exertion of descending and avoiding traps.

When we reached the final step, I turned and peered back up. The entrance was barely visible, a tiny sliver of light so far above us.

"Let's hope that door stays open long enough," Ella said.

"You had to say that, didn't you?" I asked, a shiver spreading through my body.

She laughed and poked me in the ribs. "Don't be scared, Fen. I'll protect you from the big bad door."

"Ha-ha, that's very funny." Truth was, her joking was helping calm my nerves.

This place didn't feel right at all. I could sense something within. There was something wrong, dangerous and forbidden, lurking down here. But we couldn't stop now. We were so close, and had come so far.

I moved away from the stairs and noticed a long corridor that branched off in three different directions. I shivered in the dank cold, wrinkling my nose at the musty, stale air. Thankfully, Ella's fire was helping somewhat with the chill.

"So, which way do we go?" Ella asked, annoyance written all over her face.

"I vote we try the middle first and hope none of these paths are too long," I replied, pulling out my dagger.

As we walked down the path, an ominous creak sounded further into the cave. As if a door was being opened, just out of view.

I quickly pushed Ella against the left wall and used my body as a shield against hers. I had no idea where the sound had come from but it could only mean that someone else was here, and they knew we were here.

"What do we do?" Ella whispered.

"We keep going slowly and hope whatever that was is no match for us."

"And if it is a match for us?" I could tell Ella tried to say it as a joke but the panicked edge in her voice betrayed her.

"Then we run as fast as we can and we do not look back or stop."

"I guess that's as good a plan as any." She huffed out a nervous laugh.

I took her hand in mine, caressing her fingers until some of her tension eased. We were against the wall for several more minutes before I started moving again, our hands still woven together, neither of us wanting to let go. We hadn't heard any more sounds since the creak of the door so I figured we were surely in the clear for now.

We started making our way through the middle path again. I glanced up at Ella as she dimmed the light of the fire.

"It's enough so we can see but hopefully won't alert anyone in these tunnels," she whispered and I nodded. It was smart.

The path felt like it went on and on and on with no end in sight. We had been walking for a while, our nerves making each step feel far too long, until we finally saw a wooden door off to the side of one of the cave walls. That must have been the door we heard before. Looking around I realised there was no other option but to go in there, or turn around and go back.

"You stay here and I'll go in. If you hear anything you run. I'll let you know if it's all clear." I squeezed her hand.

"No way. I'm not letting you go in there by yourself. We're in this together. Besides, you might need my fire magic." Ella went to kiss me on the cheek but I grabbed her gently by the neck and pushed her quietly up against the stone wall, claiming her mouth against my own. It was evident that since our night in the inn, neither one of us could keep our hands off of each other.

"We're in this together," I repeated her words and she smiled against my mouth.

She moved away from me and made her way to the door. I caught up with her just as she opened it. The door made the same creaking sound we heard earlier, making the hairs on my arms stand up and my skin prickle.

Her fire lit up the small room. There was a bed with a desk next to it, several potions sprawled on top and pieces of paper, some yellowed with age. The walls were lined with shelves, filled with what appeared to be ingredients for potions.

"Does a witch live here?" I whispered, mainly to myself.

"It would seem so," Ella whispered back. "But not a good one. The energy here is all wrong." Those words made me stiffen.

"I think we should quietly leave and try another path. This clearly is a dead end and not what we're after," I whispered.

I was really hoping whatever witch was down here wasn't around right now, lingering and waiting to pounce on us. The thought made my skin crawl.

"Wait... this is a dead end," Ella said.

"Yes, we established that," I replied and she rolled her eyes at me.

"No, you don't get it. We heard that door creak open." She pointed towards the wooden door. "Yet, nobody came down the path as we entered."

Realisation hit me. "The witch is still here somewhere."

The door slammed shut behind us and Ella's fire went out leaving us in pitch black.

"I knew a door was going to close on us!" Ella groaned.

"Now is not the time." I tried to move towards her but I couldn't see anything.

I heard movement within the room but I wasn't sure if it was from either of us. My heart was beating fast, trying to find my bearings.

"I can't get my fire to work," Ella said, her voice quaking.

I could tell she was close by and to the left of me so I started moving there. "It's okay, just focus. Don't panic," I answered.

My hand finally made contact with an arm, hoping it was hers.

The room suddenly lit up and I saw a fireball in Ella's hand, her eyes were peering into mine.

I saw something move from the corner of my eye. There was a figure not quite human sitting on the bed that was empty a moment ago. She had long, purple hair and the face of a beautiful woman, but her hands were hooves and her skin was grey.

"What brings you to my home," she croaked.

A cold sweat prickled at the back of my neck from her voice.

"I'm so sorry we disturbed you. We are here to collect a sword. We will get out of your way and we won't bother you again," Ella tried to reason, her voice unsteady and borderline hysterical.

"It's a little late for that, don't you think." The woman got to her feet and moved so fast I barely saw it until she was right in front of me.

"You smell off. Pungent." Her nose wrinkled.

"Well, if you move out of the way, I'll take my stench out of your space." I stood up tall and stared directly into her eyes. Trying to show I wasn't scared even though I was terrified, my heart pounding against my chest.

"You don't know what you are, do you?" Her mouth split into a terrifying grin, exposing chipped, yellow teeth.

"What is that supposed to mean?" I growled, sudden fear making my voice catch.

"What's going on?" Ella came closer and appeared ready to fight.

The woman cackled maniacally and headed towards her desk. "You'll find out soon enough. Fortunately for you, I can sense your importance to Lilith. She'd be cross with me if I harmed you."

"You work for Lilith?" I asked, confused. Witches didn't usually work with or for demons.

"Who do you think guards the sword for her? I am Abigail, Lilith's sister."

"You're lying!" Ella accused. "A demon and a witch cannot be sisters!"

"Think what you will, you ignorant witchling, but our father was a demon, our mother a witch. Lilith favours our father, I our mother. We are twins."

Ella reeled back as though she had been slapped.

"What happened to your hands?" I asked, flinching as she turned to me with a fiery gaze.

"A gift from my mother for not being as powerful as she

207

expected. More fool her though because I killed her and my sorry excuse for a father. They both rot in an eternal hell crafted by Lilith. Wonderful isn't it." She ended in a cackle.

"You said you were guarding the sword. If you give it to us we promise to leave you be and never come back to this place." I knew it was wishful thinking that she would just hand it over.

"Do you take me for a fool? I'm not giving either of you anything," she scowled.

"If you won't give us the sword and you don't want to hurt us will you let us go?" Ella crossed her arms.

"No... I don't think I will. Lilith will be pleased if I deliver you both to her personally." Abigail was now closer to the door, blocking our only way out.

She lunged for Ella and I grabbed her by the hair before she could make contact. Her head snapped back dramatically, her body following. She screamed and pushed me back into the wall. My body hit the shelves hard, glass containers shattering and falling around me.

"You destroyed my potions. You'll pay for that," she snarled, stalking towards me.

I saw Ella quickly hurl a fireball towards Abigail's leg, making contact with a sizzle and sending her falling to the ground. Her hooves would have been shredded by the glass if they were human hands. She looked up at Ella and grinned. An invisible force gripped Ella, she gasped for air as she fell to the ground, clawing at her throat.

"Stop now!" I screamed at Abigail but her grin widened further as Ella's eyes began to roll to the back of her head.

Ella's body slumped, her head hitting the ground, the flame still weakly dancing over her palm as she lost consciousness.

"I'll kill you!" I started towards her, dagger clenched in my fist.

Abigail held her hooves up and pushed them together. I felt my airway close up. I started choking, and holding my neck with one hand, trying to keep my grip on the dagger in my other hand. I began to stagger towards her. She gazed down at my runed dagger, her eyes widening. Abigail let out a shriek so loud it pierced my ears. Glass started flying around the room like a small tornado, cutting and scratching me as it passed by. Blood trickled down my face and I was becoming weaker as my lungs felt like they were going to explode. With my legs shaking, I mustered up as much strength as I could, throwing myself at Abigail and stabbing her in the neck.

She fell to the ground along with all of the glass, her air magic dissipating as she attempted to take in heaving breaths. Finally, she stopped fighting, her eyes still open but she was lifeless.

I coughed until I could finally get in a proper breath then staggered towards Ella. She was still unconscious yet her flickering flame still covered her palm, lighting the room as much as it could.

I checked her pulse and sighed in relief when I felt it strongly against my fingers. I sunk to the ground and gathered her in my arms, holding her close.

A cracking sound filled the room. The walls started to shudder, the bed shaking.

"Ella, I need you to wake up now." I brushed hair out of her face but she didn't rouse.

I got to my feet with her in my arms and made a dash for the door as rocks came tumbling down from the roof.

I just made it through the doorway and fell to the ground outside of the room with Ella, as the door was sealed shut by debris.

"What happened?" Ella asked, looking into my eyes as I held her close. Her flame that had stayed burning all this time, began to burn brighter.

My heart pounded against my chest as I pulled her in and my lips met hers. I broke the kiss after several minutes of our tongues caressing, our breathing heavy.

"The witch is dead and you're safe. I thought I lost you there for a second." I brushed my thumb across her cheek.

"You're not getting rid of me yet," Ella said with a weak smile. It was her very lame attempt at yet another joke, and it wasn't funny.

"I'm planning on having you around for a long time." I gave her a stern look.

I felt her relax into me. She put an arm around my neck and held out her hand with the flame so it wouldn't burn me. The thought of almost having lost her was replaying over and over in my head. I wrapped my arms around her waist and we stayed there for a moment, nestled in each other's arms. It was relaxing and felt like home. I didn't want it to end, but she pulled away and got to her feet slowly.

"We better get going." She brushed the dirt from the back of her pants.

I got to my feet and looked back towards the sealed door. A shiver ran down my spine, knowing Abigail's dead body was now entombed in her home forever.

"Lilith is going to be furious." Ella rubbed the back of her neck. "I don't think she will let this go."

"We'll worry about that later. We have to go find this sword and get the hell out of here before this whole place crumbles around us."

"Do you think it will?"

"Who knows. But I'm not willing to stick around longer than we need to."

CHAPTER 23

MARELLA

We both made our way back down the path we had come from, limping and holding each other close. Fenris had cuts all over his body, but he brushed me off when I offered to heal them, saying he was fine.

"Are you sure you don't want me to heal you?" I asked one last time as we walked.

"They are tiny cuts that will heal over time. Besides, you need to conserve as much energy as you can. We have no idea what we will be up against next."

"I just hate seeing you hurt."

"I know. I appreciate you wanting to heal me, I do. Let's just get through this and then we can rest and heal all we want." He ushered me down the path.

"I'll hold you to that," I smirked.

"Oh, trust me you won't have to," he laughed.

We finally made it to where the paths branched off three ways and turned to stand back in front of them.

"I think we should go left this time," Fenris said, leading me towards it.

I stopped him and he turned back to me. "No way, last time you chose we almost got killed by an evil witch sister of the Demon Queen. We're going right," I smiled and he rolled his eyes but smiled back.

We headed to the right, the path felt narrower than the last one. It also felt like we were climbing higher.

When we finally came to the end, it opened up. It was a big cave-like section that had a large opening, the sky in view.

It was more like a wide ledge. As we got closer to the edge, I gasped. It was a long way down. It was windy, the sound of it howling through the area. I took a moment to glance around, fear trickling through my veins like ice. I could feel the hairs on the back of my neck standing up. My stomach was twisted with fear because I could feel another presence in the room somewhere with us. My eyes trailed the walls until it came across the back wall.

Something was peering at us from the shadows.

I took a startled step backwards, tugging on Fenris' arm. "Fen, look!"

Looming over us was the terrifying form of a demon, a magnificent and large sword grasped in its hands. It had to be the Sword of Fatum.

Fenris startled, the same way I had, but quickly recovered, stepping forward. "He's trapped in there!"

And he was. The demon was frozen, encased in some kind of clear, hard substance that I didn't recognise. It resembled crystal.

"How are we meant to get the sword?" I groaned.

"We're going to have to somehow break him out of there. It's the only way to get it," Fenris replied, looking around the cave.

I created a second ball of fire with my other hand and threw it at the entombed demon in an attempt to melt it away. It didn't even leave a scorch mark.

I shrugged my shoulders. "Well, I'm fresh out of ideas."

I moved around the cave while Fenris moved around the opposite direction but there was nothing that could help, it was completely bare of any resources. There wasn't even a rock or some stones, it was just the demon and sword, encased in this crystal like substance, on a wide ledge.

Fenris moved towards the crystal and ran his hand along it. "Shit," he gasped as he held out his hand that was now bleeding. "Be careful, it's really sharp apparently."

The room shook violently, as if there was an earthquake. I staggered to the side, my shoulder connecting painfully with the cave wall.

I grabbed Fenris by the arm and pulled him away as we watched in terrified fascination. The weird crystal encasing started to dissolve around the demon and sword before our eyes.

"What the hell. Did your blood do that?" I asked.

"I... I have no idea. Maybe it's a tremor from the witch's room collapsing," Fenris replied, stumbling backwards.

There was a loud cracking sound as the demon burst free of the final shards of his prison. He loomed over us, raising the sword and pointing it at Fenris' chest. We started to slowly back away.

The stench of the demon made me gag, he smelt of rotten eggs. I guess that's what happens when you're stuck in a crystal form for too long.

Now that he was out of his prison we could see him better. He was twice the size of Fenris with eyes as blue as sapphires, a red ring around both of the irises and scale-like skin the colour of the night sky.

He let out a roar that shook the cave and began barrelling towards us. Fenris pushed me out of the way and shielded me with his body. The sword hit the wall with a loud clang. A sharp pain shot through my ankle as I got to my feet. I summoned a shield of fire in front of us and threw it at the demon. His scales lit up with the heat of my fire, but the demon grinned and made his way towards us. It was clear that my magic wasn't going to be much help at all in this situation.

"Stop!" Fenris roared.

The demon halted suddenly in his tracks, Fenris and I both panting at the fact we were almost demon fodder. But why did he stop because of Fenris? I looked over at him, trying to make sense of it.

The demon lifted his sword again and we moved apart just in time as it came crashing down on the ground.

"Do you work for Lilith?" he demanded in a loud, monstrous voice.

"We're enemies of Lilith," I answered loudly.

The demon held the sword in front of him ready to attack but he didn't swing it again. "I'm guessing you're after the sword then?"

"Yes. We are here for the sword." Fenris gulped. "What happened to you?"

The demon paused for a moment, narrowing his terrifying

eyes. Finally, he said, "Lilith put me here. I tried to use the sword on her to change her destiny and she tried to steal it from me. I wouldn't let her take it. Her only option was to imprison me with the sword and leave me here to rot."

"If you're no friend of Lilith, will you help us kill her?" Fenris asked, I looked up at him.

"You swear you aren't in league with her?" The demon's eyes looked exhausted.

"We want her gone. If it helps you trust us, we just killed her sister." Fenris answered.

"You both killed Abigail?"

"Her body is entombed in her room if you want to go look," I said, matter-of-factly.

"I don't doubt you did. Even entombed in my prison I felt the cave shake." He grunted. "I will give you the sword and I'll even get you home, but after that I'm leaving. I'm sorry, but I can't face her again, I need to get away as far as I can," the demon said.

The fact that this strong demon was scared of Lilith made me even more frightened. "I understand. Thank you for agreeing to take us home."

"I'm Brackas, by the way." The demon pressed his hand against his chest.

"I'm Ella and this is Fenris," I answered, pointing from me to Fenris.

"How did you know Lilith?" Fenris asked.

"I was one of her soldiers and one of her friends, or so I thought." He sighed and looked off into the distance. "She had my mate and daughter murdered right in front of me because we tried to leave her inner circle. We don't all want to be bad, some of us are good, or try to be. Some of us just want to live our lives as normal as we can."

I covered my mouth, tears welling in my eyes for this demon. "I'm so sorry that happened, Brackas."

"I did some bad things when I was younger but I stopped wanting to be that demon a long time ago. Lilith didn't like that. She has and always will be pure evil."

I was shocked at what I was hearing. Demons weren't all evil. Was that truly possible? All we knew about them was that they were savage and destroyed anything they touched. How was it possible they had the capacity to care, to love, to feel? I was a witch who was constantly worried about Witch Hunters and chastised them for assuming we were all evil beings, yet here I was, learning we had been doing the exact same thing to demons.

"How are you going to take us home?" Fenris cleared his throat.

The demon smiled and handed Fenris the sword and the sheath from his back, then he walked towards the edge of the ledge and looked out into the world. The sun shone down on Brackas. He closed his eyes and basked in it. We had been in this cave for so long.

"I've missed this." The demon breathed in and out then opened his eyes again and turned around.

Fenris and I moved towards him. I had never been this close to one without the need to fight for my life. It was so new and interesting. I wondered what this could mean for the world. Were there other demons that were just like this one?

"Are you ready to go?" Brackas asked.

"How do we do this?" Fenris sheathed the sword on his back.

"Climb up when I change."

"Change to what?" I asked.

But he didn't answer. Instead he changed from a demon into a creature that resembled a dragon, his wings breaking free of his scales and unfurling, his neck stretching, face elongating into a snout and a tail whipping out behind him. He was large enough to carry both of us on his back. His scales now made a lot of sense. His wings were so large they almost didn't fit inside the cave.

"Woah," I gasped.

"Did you know demon's could do that?" Fenris asked me.

"I had no idea," I answered, my mouth still open.

"Are you two going to climb on or continue staring?" Brackas spoke.

That startled me. I had no idea a dragon could talk. Hell, I had no idea there were demons that could turn into dragons. I always wondered where they came from but you didn't hear much about dragons. I didn't even think anyone in our lifetime had seen one, until today of course. Sure, they were written about in books but it was always assumed to be a myth.

Fenris jumped onto Brackas' wing and helped me up. We climbed then made our way onto his back where his neck started. We got into a comfortable, safe position and Fenris held onto what he could while I held onto him.

"Ready to fly?" Brackas asked.

"As ready as we'll ever be," I answered.

Brackas spread out his wings as much as he could then dropped. We were plummeting at such a fast pace I thought for sure we were about to hit the ground or fall off, but all of a sudden we got pulled up and finally started gliding at a peaceful pace.

"This is beyond words," Fenris yelled out over the wind.

"What, you've never ridden a dragon before?" Brackas

asked.

"I think I can say with confidence that nobody has ridden a dragon before," Fenris replied.

"You'd be surprised what your ancestors got up to." Brackas veered right towards our town.

"What are we going to do once we get to Hayselwood?" I asked.

"I think we should go see Greta first before we go anywhere near your home. We know what could potentially happen to you there, so let's not tempt fate too soon. Let's get a plan in place," Fenris replied.

"Good idea."

***

The sun was shining high in the sky when Brackas began descending towards Hayselwood. Surprisingly, it was a very calm landing right on the outskirts of the Aldar and Fraying forests that lead into our town.

"How do we know nobody saw you? That people won't start talking about dragons?" Fenris asked as we hopped off Brackas' back.

"It's amazing what you can get away with when you're invisible," Brackas answered.

"But we can still see you?" I furrowed my eyebrows.

"Well, I don't need to be invisible to you! I was also able to make both of you invisible because you were both touching me," he replied. "It would have been weird seeing two humans floating high in the sky," he added as he bowed his head, laughing. "Thank you for freeing me by the way."

"Thank you for the sword and for getting us home safely," I

said, a smile crossing my face.

"I do have a question before you leave." Fenris moved towards Brackas.

"Go ahead."

"Why did my blood free you?"

"I could smell her on you. When you freed me I could smell her. That's why I thought you were working for Lilith."

"Wait, what?" I moved forward so I was standing next to Fenris.

"Why would you smell her on me?" Fenris asked.

"Her blood flows through your veins, Fenris." Brackas looked from Fenris to me. "Do you really not get it yet?"

"Get what?" I was starting to lose patience.

"Lilith is your mother! That's the only reason for your blood to smell like her. The only reason you would have been able to dissolve the prison for me that she created with Abigail. Nobody else but her offspring or them could do that," Brackas answered.

Fenris paled and stepped back, looking wide eyed at the ground.

How could this even be true? Fenris was Lilith's son. The same Lilith who was going to kill me. And I was falling for him, I made love to him. Did this mean Fenris was part demon?

"There is something else you must know," Brackas said.

The way his voice deepened sent a shiver down my spine. "What is it?" I asked.

"It is said that Lilith is destined to destroy the world. I assume that's why you wanted it but you need to make sure you stab her in the heart for it to work. It's why I had the sword, to stop her so I could make sure my family was safe. I guess in the end it never mattered."

My eyes widened and I opened my mouth. "Actually, it was my destiny we were wanting to change. Lilith is going to kill me. I saw it from a Scree Demon's vision."

Brackas grunted. "I'm sorry to hear that. But you must use the sword on Lilith. If she destroys the world we are all dead." He bowed his dragon head. "I must go. But I wish you both good luck. Give her my regards when you drive that sword into her, will you?" Brackas bowed his head one more time before turning around and flying off into the beautiful morning sky, leaving Fen and I with our world falling apart around us.

CHAPTER 24

FENRIS

I was a... what? A demon. How could that be? How could it be possible that I had Lilith's blood running through my veins? I was going to be sick, I could feel the bile rising in my throat. I turned from Ella and fell to the ground, throwing up, sweat lacing my brows. I wiped my mouth against my shirt and got back up.

"Are you alright, Fen?" Ella asked as she approached me.

"Stay away from me!" I cried out, backing away.

"Fen, please." Her eyes were pleading.

I interrupted before she could say more. "No! I don't want to hurt you."

"You're not going to hurt me. I trust you." Ella carefully moved forward, but stopped when I backed away again. "You haven't hurt me before, you've given me no reason not to trust you, Fen. Come on."

"I don't trust myself anymore. I'm a... how can I be a... I don't understand." I choked on my words.

"Have you ever felt different?" Ella questioned.

"You mean have I ever felt like a demon? No, I've never felt out of the ordinary at all."

"Maybe you never inherited demonic powers then. Maybe the human in you is too strong." She was trying to comfort me.

I started walking, Ella following close behind. "I need to figure out who I am and how Lilith is my... my mother. Does she even know about me?"

"All good questions and we can figure it out, but first we need to get to Greta."

"Wait, Ella. She's destined to kill you. Which means we'll be seeing her soon. I can't... I don't know how to live with this information." My body felt like it was on fire, my blood boiling inside of me. Everything I was learning made me feel uncomfortable in my own skin.

"It'll be okay, Fen. We'll figure it out. Even if it means you don't come with me to face her."

I cut her off. "That's not an option at all. You will not face this alone. I am with you every step of the way, you hear me?" She nodded at that.

I was so consumed by my thoughts of what Brackas told me about Lilith that I had completely forgotten what he said about Ella.

"If we use the sword on Lilith that means we won't change your destiny. She may still kill you." I stopped and looked up at her, still trying to maintain a distance.

"I know, but what choice do we have? We can't spare my life just for the world to be destroyed. I'll die anyway and then what was the point?" She looked at the ground. I could see a tear welling up in her eye.

"I won't let you risk your life. We do what we were always planning to do."

"No, Fenris! We can't be selfish. Promise me you'll help take Lilith down, no matter what?"

Hearing her name, knowing that it was my mother, made me want to throw up all over again. But Ella was right, we couldn't let the world be destroyed.

"I don't want this. I need you." I moved towards her, tears slipping down my cheek.

"I know, Fen. But you don't need me. You never have. You just need to believe in yourself. Believe that you're better than all of this." Ella wrapped her arms around me and laid her head on my shoulder. "Make the world a better place, Fen."

Her body began to shake as she cried and I tried to hold more of my own tears back so I could be strong for her. I needed her to know I was here for her and I'd be her armour for as long as I could be.

She pulled away and I brushed her tears with my thumbs. "I don't want to lose you, Ella. To lose this."

I pressed my lips against hers and relished in the taste of her, the intoxicating taste that I would miss for the rest of my life. How was I going to be strong enough to let her go?

I pulled away, both of us panting. Left longing for more.

"I love you, Fenris," she breathed.

"I love you, Ella." I placed my forehead against hers.

We both knew what needed to be done but we stood there in each other's arms, our foreheads still pressed together for several more minutes.

I sighed as she moved away and looked towards Hayselwood.

"We have to go now," she whispered.

I gulped. "Okay."

I took the sword from my back then opened my pack and removed a blanket. I wrapped the blanket around the sword and held it close to me. I couldn't risk losing it or anyone seeing me with it.

She grasped my hand as we walked towards Hayselwood.

Ella was admirable and strong. Brave in the face of what we were going to do. I looked over at her as we walked and she held her head high. I thought of her kindness, the way she was always selfless and tried to help everyone else. She was still by my side despite the news of Lilith, even in the face of her own fate. Knowing Lilith was the one destined to take her life. I loved her more than I ever knew was possible to love someone and I knew my whole world would be destroyed once she was gone. But I had to be just as strong as her, for her. I had to be selfless too and I had to help everyone.

We were entering Hayselwood when I stopped Ella and turned her towards me. "I need to go speak with the King before we head into danger. He was the one who found me. I need to know if he knew Lilith. Did you want to come with me?" I grabbed her hand and held it up to my chest.

She smiled but I could see the pain behind it. "You go do what you have to, Fen. I'll go see Greta while you're there. If you see her let her know I'll wait for her in the tavern."

"I can do that. But what if something happens while we're apart?" My heart started beating so hard I thought it was going to rip out of my chest.

"I won't go near the cottage without you. I'll be fine. We'll meet at the tavern later."

I gently kissed the side of her lips, my heart fluttering. We gave one last sad smile to each other before separating, her walking towards the tavern and me walking towards the church. I needed to tell Greta to meet Ella then I needed to acquire a horse to get to the castle.

As I was walking up the stairs to the church I felt a hand on my shoulder. Turning around, I came face to face with Logan.

He tapped his foot on the ground, his arms crossed. "You've been gone for a while. Are you ready to explain what's going on?"

CHAPTER 25

FENRIS

"Logan, I'm sorry I really don't have time right now," I pleaded.

I continued to walk up the stairs, the sword still hidden under the blanket I was clutching to my chest, but Logan grabbed my arm and pulled me down. "You will make the time. I'm not your best friend right now, Fenris. I'm your leader. You will report to me!" his voice rose, anger lacing his tone.

My stomach churned as I swallowed a lump in my throat. We had never kept anything from each other before, but now I had so many secrets, so much to hide from him. The truth about Ella ... the truth about me.

Every truth had the potential to put both of us in danger ... well, more danger than we were already in.

"Alright, fine. But can we do it somewhere more private?" I

gestured towards the church doors.

Logan looked me up and down, his eyes landing on the blanket. "What's that?"

"I'll explain it all to you when we're in a more private setting, please, Logan," I pleaded.

He cleared his throat. "You have half an hour to meet me in my office. Go wash up, you look and smell horrible. Do not go anywhere else until you have seen me. I mean it, Fen. I'll see you soon." I saw a glimmer of my friend before he ascended the stairs. I just hoped it stayed that way once I told him my secrets.

I had no idea how I was going to make this right. What could I tell him? How could I make him even begin to understand that I was helping to save the life of a witch, that I was falling for her. I wasn't sure he could understand.

On my way to my bedroom I saw Greta sitting on one of the seats near a window off to the side. She glanced up as I approached and smiled.

"Oh, Fenris. How are you?" She placed the book beside her and stood.

"I'm alright. I can't talk too much, I have to go get ready for a meeting with Logan. But Ella is waiting for you in the tavern to tell you everything."

"I'll leave immediately, thank you." She went to walk away but turned back. "Logan may be angry at the moment but he's just worried about you."

"How do you know?" I furrowed my eyebrows.

"Well... Logan and I... we've been spending a lot of time together, getting to know each other," she answered.

"Oh! That's great news!" I smiled, truly feeling happy for them both. "Thank you, Greta. I just hope I can think of something to say to him." I bowed my head. "I'm glad he's got you. You're good for him."

She blushed. "You might be surprised at what he can handle. Just be cautious with what you share but just know that he could potentially be trusted with Ella."

I nodded then we both turned and went our separate ways.

I walked at a fast pace to my bedroom, trying not to draw too much attention to myself. I didn't have much time to bathe and get to Logan's office.

***

I stood in front of Logan's office door, knowing I needed to get the conversation over with but still unsure what I was supposed to say to him. Would he understand or would he tell the King and shun me? Stripping me of my Witch Hunter title. Would I be cast out of the castle and all I've ever known?

I was so nervous about how he'd react but I had no other choice. I had to tell him the truth. I gave him my word I would and I'd never been the type of person to break my promises. Besides, he was like a brother to me and I didn't want to betray that relationship by continuing to keep things from him. I had to be honest and hope for the best. No matter what happened next I'd know I'd done everything in my power to help Ella and that I was honest with everyone I love.

I knocked at the door and heard Logan's voice telling me to come in. I hesitated for a moment then opened the door and took a seat opposite him.

"Are you ready to tell me what is going on?" he asked as he leant forward and placed his hands on his desk.

I exhaled a breath heavily, preparing myself for what was

about to happen.

"Listen, Logan... What I'm about to tell you may seem a bit out there but I need you to have an open mind and I need you to trust me. Know that I would never put us in danger." I laced my fingers together and squeezed my hands, my heart hammering in my chest.

Logan furrowed his eyebrows. "Okay, go on."

"You remember Ella right? The girl who saved Greta's life?"

"Yes I remember her. Why?" his right eyebrow rose.

"That trip I went on ... that was with her."

He smiled. "Fenris, you're seeing someone. This is great news. Why would I ever be mad about that? You could have told me from the start that this is what you were doing."

"It's more than just seeing each other. But that's not what this is about." I stood up and walked towards his bookcase.

I was finding it hard to keep looking him in the eyes when I was about to drop something huge into his lap.

"Ella... Ella is... well, she's a witch." I froze, waiting for his response.

"She's a... what?" he gasped.

"She's not a bad witch, I swear it. She's a good person and there's this vision she had of her death and I've been trying to help find a way to save her." I was talking fast, trying to get all my reasoning out before he could say anything.

"You've been fraternising with our enemy this whole time?" Logan growled. "What were you thinking, Fenris?"

"It's not what you think, Logan. She's not evil."

"She's a witch, Fenris. They are all vile creatures," he spat.

"Logan, we've not met many witches, but if you recall the coven we encountered not long ago, to those witches, to that little girl, we were the evil ones." I stepped towards him. "She was a child, Logan, woken to find her family being slaughtered and we did the same to her. *We* are the monsters under the bed to them." I choked on my words, feeling my chest tighten.

"I can't believe what I'm hearing right now. We were punishing them for their crimes, Fenris!"

"What crimes, Logan? For being witches? Something they did not choose to be, but were born as."

Logan looked away. "How do you know Ella hasn't been using you this whole time to bring down the Witch Hunters?"

"Ella isn't like that. She saved Lyra from a higher demon when she could have just let her die."

"Yet, you still felt the need to keep all of this from me... because you knew what you were doing was wrong!" he yelled.

"It's not wrong! I love her!" The power of my confession to him threatened to overwhelm me.

Logan scoffed, shaking his head. "You need to get out, I can't even look at you right now. I can't deal with this."

"Logan, please-"

"GET OUT!"

I stumbled backwards, fumbling for the door handle and escaping my best friend ... well, perhaps no longer my best friend.

I'd just told him only part of the truth, and all I'd done was infuriate him, putting Ella in grave danger.

How could Logan not put any trust in me over this? After all we'd been through? He knew my feelings about being a Witch Hunter, to an extent. I had said as much when we took down that coven. He must have suspected I didn't agree with what we were doing to witches.

I raced to my room and gathered my things. My sword, the Sword of Fatum that was still wrapped in a blanket, my pistols and my daggers.

I closed my bedroom door behind me. Something about it felt final. Like I would never be here again, in this church.

I turned to walk away and almost jumped out of my skin to see Andras standing right in front of me. His eyes bored into mine.

"You're back," he remarked.

"Andras, I haven't seen you in so long. I'm in a bit of a hurry so unfortunately I can't catch up right now." I went to walk away, nervously laughing.

Andras wrenched my arm back. "I know you and Logan are up to something that involves me somehow. Do you both think I'm stupid?" he whispered in my ear.

"I don't know what you're talking about. Now let me go." I yanked my arm away.

He held his hands up in front of him. "Fine... fine. But I know you are both trying to get rid of me. I guess I'll just have to get rid of you both first." he smirked as he walked away.

Another thing I'd have to deal with when all of this was over, when Lilith was taken care of. I'd make sure to tell Logan and help him come up with a plan of action. Whether he hated me or not, he was still my friend and these people, the Witch Hunters, still meant something to me. I'd be damned if I saw harm come to any of them.

As I was about to walk out the church doors I was stopped by a castle worker.

"I'm glad you're back, Sir. Princess Lyra sent me to find you, and said you should surely be back by now. She is asking for you, Sir," she said.

Could I not be left alone for two seconds? I needed to get to the castle to talk to the King then meet with Ella, I didn't have time to deal with anything else.

"Can you tell her I don't have time right now and will see her later today," I answered, heading out the door towards the stairs.

The girl called out to me. "She said it's urgent, sir."

I closed my eyes for a moment, sighed then opened them again. I groaned, making my way to the stables. I quickly saddled a horse, placing my sword and the Sword of Fatum under the blanket on the horse's back. Climbing into the saddle, I knocked my feet against the horse's side. We galloped down the streets all the way to the castle.

***

Lyra was sitting on her couch by the fire when I arrived, a shawl wrapped around her shoulders.

"Lyra, what's going on?" I asked, taking a seat.

"Fen, it's bad news. Valdori plans to attack Crayton soon. I sent George to see the triplets and they think we need to start preparing for the worst. Their forces are strong." Her eyebrows creased, her voice frantic.

"Lyra, have you told the King?" I was breathless with worry.

"No, I was hoping you could come with me to talk to him. He will be so angry with me."

"Why did you keep all of this from him? He could have been preparing this whole time, mustering his army. You've potentially doomed this kingdom." My voice rose.

Lyra flinched. "I don't know, I think I just wanted to try and get actual proof. You don't get it, Fenris. I'm just a silly Princess. Who would believe a word that comes out of my mouth?"

"You should have more faith in your father, your King. What's he going to say when he finds out you've been keeping this from him the whole time?" I questioned her, my frustration with the whole situation boiling over. I had no patience left to be gentle with her.

"I don't know, okay! I thought I could handle this by myself, gather the intel and evidence I needed then present it to the King. Show him I'm more than just a Princess stuck in her castle."

"But that's what you are, Lyra. You're a Princess. You're the future ruler of this kingdom and you need to grow up and realise that this isn't how you're going to be able to do things once you step into that role as Queen."

"I don't want to be Queen! I hate being stuck in this stupid castle and I hate not being able to go on adventures like the rest of you," she complained.

I was getting exhausted with this argument and her childish behaviour. It was always a constant with her.

"These aren't just adventures, Lyra. These are quests with a purpose. Life or death situations. We aren't just having fun and sitting around, we are doing what needs to be done."

"What do you think I've been doing with the triplets? I've been trying to do what needs to be done."

"If you were doing that you would have told the King by now."

She lowered her head. "I'm sorry."

"Dammit, Lyra this is serious and I have other places to be. I'm sick of you acting like a child, being irresponsible and making messes we all have to waste our time cleaning up."

Tears began to stream down her face. "I will go tell the King now."

"I'll come with you."

"No, don't do me any favours, Fenris. You can leave, go do whatever it is you were doing."

I slowly exhaled a breath through my mouth as I softened and moved towards her. I gave her a hug as my anger began to dissipate. "I'm sorry, Lyra. I didn't mean to upset you. I will come with you to talk to him but we do have to be quick. Ella could be in danger right now."

"What's happened?" Lyra wiped the tears from her eyes and cheeks.

"Well, I told Logan what she is and he kicked me out. He took it worse than I could ever have imagined."

"Of course he did, Fen. He doesn't understand," she said solemnly.

"I need to hurry back to her before Logan calls a witch hunt."

"Do you really think he'd do that?" Lyra gasped.

"He was furious, Lyra. I think he absolutely is capable of it."

"Okay, well let's go get this over with so you can leave."

**

"Come in," King Aldric called through the closed door of his council room.

Lyra and I made our way in when the guards opened the door. They closed it behind us, sealing us in. We both took a seat at the long table.

"What can I help you both with?" the King asked.

"Father, we have something important to tell you." Lyra placed her hands on the table. "I have been gathering information to bring to you regarding Valdori. My spies believe we will be under attack soon. We should prepare. It's bad, I don't know how close they are and..."

The King laughed, interrupting her. "I have already started preparing, daughter."

"Wait... you know?" I asked, looking up.

"Of course I know. You think I don't keep an eye on Valdori? I am the King. It's my duty to ensure my kingdom is safe."

"It's my duty too as the Princess." Lyra paused. "Father, I wish to fight," Lyra said.

That was surprising and unexpected. I knew she wanted adventure, but I had no idea she wanted to actually fight. The thought was ridiculous, she had never trained to fight a day in her life.

"You will do no such thing. You will stay in the castle and look after the women and children. Escape if it ever comes to that. *That* is your duty as Princess."

"I don't want to sit back while our people die," she cried out.

"I don't really care what you wish to do, Lyra. As your King, I order it."

She crossed her arms and fell back into her seat. "What do you plan to do about the Demon Queen then? Lilith is working with Valdori," Lyra retorted.

King Aldric glanced towards me, his eyes searching mine, then quickly looked away.

My eyes widened. "You knew, didn't you?"

"What are you talking about, Fenris?" The King poured himself a drink.

"You knew that Lilith was my mother, didn't you?"

Lyra peered at me, her mouth open. "Wait, what?"

King Aldric drank the contents of his cup, his eyes looking anywhere but at me.

"Why did you never tell me?" I got to my feet.

"Did you really think knowing this would have helped you in any way, growing up?" the King challenged.

"Do you know who my father is?" I ignored his question.

King Aldric's forehead crinkled and his lips turned down into a frown.

"He's dead, isn't he?" I questioned, wanting to know the whole truth.

Lyra glanced between me and the King, her mouth still open.

"He isn't dead," the King finally answered.

"Who is he then?"

"Fenris, please-" the King started.

"ANSWER ME NOW!" I yelled.

I couldn't believe I had just spoken to the King like that but I needed to know and I was sick of being lied to. He surprisingly didn't anger or flinch. King Aldric got to his feet and came towards me.

"I'm your father, Fenris." He placed his hand over my shoulder.

Chills washed over my whole body, my feet almost coming out from under me at his revelation.

Lyra gasped. "Father, what are you talking about?"

The King sighed, removing his hand from my shoulder. "I met Lilith before she was a Queen, when she was part of the Demon King's inner circle, a high demon." He started pacing the room. "It was before I married your mother, Lyra. I want to make it clear that I loved Carmel fiercely. When she got sick and died it broke me, I still feel like a part of my soul is missing." He cleared his throat. "But I also loved Lilith, I truly did. Maybe not as much as Carmel, but the feelings were there and they were real. Lilith fell pregnant with you, Fenris." He turned to look at Lyra and I. "But the second she had you she told me she was going to take down the Demon King so she needed me to protect you. I took you from her and I didn't plan to give you back. She was a high demon, I would not allow my son to be taken into her world. When she found out she was angry... furious."

"Why didn't she ever come and get me?"

"Because she is unable to get into the castle thanks to the Witch Hunter runes engraved into the walls. We worked tirelessly to ensure the castle was completely protected to keep you safe," he explained.

"But I'm not always within the castle walls, she could have gotten me at any time."

"I sent word to her that you had died so she would stop wanting for you. We even sent her the body of a dead child that resembled you. The runes prevented her from inspecting the castle, she had no choice but to take our word for it. There was no other evidence to prove otherwise."

I covered my mouth. "You killed a child?"

"No, Fenris, I did not kill a child. We used the body of a child that was already deceased," he said, his tone short with me.

"Is this why she has joined forces with Valdori? To take you down for what you did?" Lyra screeched.

"It would appear so," the King responded.

"You should be ashamed of yourself." Lyra threw her hands up. She walked towards the doors, storming out after the guards on this side opened them for her.

I went to leave too but turned around as I got to the door. "I can't believe all these years you let me think I had no parents, no family."

"We have always been your family whether you knew it was by blood or not, Fenris," he said simply, as though it made up

238

for everything.

I turned and made my way out the door. I didn't want to listen to anything else he had to say. I went from not knowing who my parents were, having no blood related family to finding out I was a bastard Prince. My father was the King, my mother was a Demon Queen and Lyra... she was my half sister.

I couldn't think about it anymore. I needed to get to Ella before Logan potentially called a witch hunt or even before Ella went back to her cottage without me. She was my first priority. Nothing else mattered to me at that moment. I had to know she was going to be okay even after everything I'd learnt about myself. I ran out of the castle, got on my horse and raced for the tavern.

As I approached the town there were people screaming everywhere, running away from the tavern, hiding behind buildings. I heard someone scream about a demon attack.

I got off the horse and removed my sword and the Sword of Fatum from underneath the blanket. I sheathed the Sword of Fatum to my back and clutched my runed sword tightly in my hand, holding it up ready for a fight.

"FENRIS!" I heard a voice scream.

I swung around and saw Greta running for me, breathless and clutching her chest.

"Greta, what's going on?" I grabbed hold of her just as she barreled into me.

"It's Ella. A demon took her!" She was out of breath.

"Where?" I looked around at the now deserted town, it was quiet and eerie.

"The tavern. He burst through the tavern. She told me to come find you."

"Go back to the church and be careful. Stay safe, Greta."

"He said Lilith sent him. It's happening isn't it?" Her eyes welled up.

"Just go and know that I will do everything in my power to keep her safe."

Greta let go of me and ran for the church.

I moved closer to the tavern and noticed the back door was open. I walked inside and the destruction was horrific.

The front door was gone and the inside was trashed. I stepped inside and found tables destroyed, barely more than splinters left, the bar was slashed by what appeared to be enormous claws. What I didn't find was any sign of Ella.

CHAPTER 26

MARELLA

I made my way to the tavern hoping that I would eventually find Greta there. I had to avoid the cottage for as long as I possibly could. I didn't know when everything was going to happen but I had a feeling it would be soon. It loomed over me like a darkness I couldn't shake.

I walked through the tavern doors and ordered an ale at the bar. When it was ready I made my way down to our usual area. I drank while I waited for what felt like forever and was about to get up when I finally saw Greta enter the tavern. She went to the bar, got two drinks and headed towards me.

"I saw Fenris and he said you'd be here. He was heading off to see Logan," Greta said as she took a seat.

"Wait... he's going to see Logan? He was meant to go speak to the King."

"I'm not sure sorry. Why was he going to see the King? What's going on?" she asked.

I explained everything to her that had happened as we drank together. About our trip to Hunterville, the bandits, the fortune teller. How we managed to get into the cave. The fact Lilith had a sister and we had killed her. She listened but looked on with concern.

"Wait, Lilith had a sister? That's very interesting," she speculated.

"We learnt a lot on our trip." I took a long drink of my ale. "You haven't even heard the craziest parts. Some demons can turn into dragons."

"Woah, dragons. Seriously?"

"There is something else too." I cleared my throat. "Lilith... She's Fenris' mother."

Her eyes widened as her drink paused against her lips. "Excuse me, what? That's... wow. How is Fenris after learning that?" Greta asked.

"He's not doing too well. That's why he wanted to speak to the King. He thinks he may know something about it. After all, the King was the one who apparently found him and brought him to the castle when he was younger."

"Wow. That's massive news. Poor Fen. So, where do you go from here?"

"I'm trying to avoid the cottage as much as I can. Besides, Fenris still has the sword so I can't go without him anyway," I explained.

"I get that. I hope everything works out. I'm so scared for you, Ella." She furrowed her eyebrows and frowned as she grasped my hand.

I tried to change the subject. "Anyway, how are things here?"

"Well, as you know, Logan took me on as his scholar." She was blushing.

"How is it? Being the Witch Hunter leader's scholar," I asked.

"He's very... he's a gentleman. He's always looking out for me while we are out. I know Witch Hunters are supposed to take care of their scholars but I don't know, it feels like he cares for me."

"Do you care for him in return?" I asked, smirking.

"I think I actually might. I'm not sure if it'll lead to anything but I do hope it could," she answered.

"This is wonderful news, Greta. After everything you've been through you deserve to be happy."

"What of your happiness, Ella? Before you even left I saw the way you and Fenris looked at each other. Is there something there?" She took another swig of her drink and I did the same.

"Things have definitely progressed in our relationship." I hid my face behind my drink.

"You've got to tell me now." Greta smiled.

"We may have ... done some things. We also said 'I love you' to each other." I blushed.

"Well, as soon as we get this Lilith business out of the way we can deal with both of our love lives," Greta said and we both laughed. "I have some news for you actually."

I straightened up in my seat. "What is it?"

"Andras is back. He has been home for a while now. He arrived not long after you both left actually." Greta bit her bottom lip.

"You're kidding me! Has he come near you?"

"Thankfully he has kept his distance. I think he knows something is up."

I massaged both my temples, feeling a headache coming on.

"That's not good. What does Logan say?"

She smiled. "Logan has been amazing. He has Andras running all over the place to try and keep him as busy as possible so he doesn't even have time to do anything."

"I still don't understand why they can't just get rid of him already."

"They unfortunately lack the proof needed to convict him. The King would question why he was relieved of his duties so Logan needs to make sure he has evidence."

I shook my head. "The quicker they get rid of him the better."

"I agree. Unfortunately he's been on his best behaviour. I think he knows he's being watched." Greta sighed.

I grasped her hand in mine. "We'll get him soon. He will slip up eventually and they'll have no choice but to remove him. If I know anything about Andras it's that he can't help himself."

I removed my hand from Greta's and was just about to get up to get us some more drinks when we were both thrown off our chairs, our bodies crashing into the wall as the front of the tavern exploded inwards, and in loomed a demon that I had seen before.

It was the high demon Fenris had killed to save me. The one that overturned the Princess' carriage. How was he alive? I had never seen a demon come back to life. He looked around the room until his eyes landed on me and his mouth lifted into a grin.

"YOU!" he roared in a deep, dark voice.

Everyone started panicking, running around screaming. They all tried to scramble out the back entrance of the tavern. I got to my feet and Greta came to stand beside me.

"How are you alive?" I gasped. "I saw you die!"

"Higher demons don't die you stupid witch. We get sent

back down to Lilith." The demon's deep voice made my bones shudder.

He lumbered towards us, knocking tables aside and crushing chairs, careless of the destruction he wrought on the tavern, now empty, except for Greta and I. And a large, violent higher demon.

I moved to put myself between Greta and the demon, summoning as much fierceness as I could. "What do you want?"

"Lilith sent me to retrieve you. She's waiting. She told me to let you know she has Hulda." The demon laughed.

"Hulda," I whispered. "You better not have hurt her."

"She's fine... for now. But if you don't come with me... well, that's another story."

"I'll come. Just leave my friends alone. Leave Hulda alone. Lilith will get what she wants."

I still had no clue what she wanted with me. Why would she want to kill me? Maybe I destroyed too many of her demons over the years or maybe she was killing off witches. Who knew? I guess I'd find out soon. I had to hurry, not knowing what state Hulda was in made my heart race and my breath catch.

Greta grasped my arm as I tried to leave. "You can't go with that thing, Ella. You don't have the sword," she whispered through gritted teeth.

I detangled her clawing fingers from my skin, hissing urgently. "Don't worry about me, just find Fen. Tell him what's happening."

She gave me a wild-eyed look, and I scowled. "GO!" I snapped, and with a terrified nod, she raced for the back door. I approached the demon, fear racing through my body.

As I got close enough he grabbed me and tossed me over his massive shoulder, stomping out of the tavern and heading in the direction of the forest.

The direction of my home.

CHAPTER 27

FENRIS

There was only one place she could possibly be. I had to make my way to her home, to the cottage. I had the Sword of Fatum strapped to my back and I was ready. Ready to face Lilith, my mother. Ready to use the sword on her just like Ella wanted. We had to stop her from destroying the world. It was going to be the hardest thing I'd ever done, I ever would do, but I had to be strong and I had to face it, face those fears and face Lilith ... face Ella's fated death.

I mounted my horse, kicking him into a gallop and headed for the Fraying Forest. I only hoped I wasn't too late to see Ella, to change Lilith's destiny of destroying the world. I would never forgive myself if I didn't make things right.

The demon had left destruction in his path, buildings were burning and crops were nothing but scorched, black patches.

The path had cracks and splits where it was once smooth.

As the horse galloped through the Fraying Forest, branches were hitting me in the face, twigs snagging on my shirt but I didn't care, I needed to get to Ella now.

I made it to her cottage and the door had been blasted in, pieces of splintered wood littering the ground.

"Ella!" I screamed as I leapt off of the horse.

I burst through the opening of the cottage, coming up short when I noticed Ella's too-still body slumped on the floor.

"She's not dead, Witch Hunter."

I glanced up, shock pulsing in my veins as I met the eyes of the demon we had killed the night Ella saved Lyra.

"Well, she's not dead, yet," the demon added, a gruesome smirk twisting his already ugly face.

Behind him, Hulda was tied to a chair, mouth gagged and head lolling.

I took a step closer to Ella, but a force held me back. Smoke coalesced between us, and a figure started to materialise within it.

She wore a black dress with a black train trailing down that stopped to her ankles. She had black horns protruding from her head and long, flowing red hair.

Lilith.

"What have you done to her?" I cried out.

Lilith smirked, then flicked a hand in the demon's direction. "That will be all. Leave us."

With a bow of his head he vanished.

"And who are you?" Lilith purred, stalking towards me. I felt frozen to the spot as she trailed a claw-like nail down my cheek.

"I shouldn't be surprised you don't know your own son." I

gritted my teeth.

"Excuse me?" she seethed.

"Can you not smell it on me?" I gestured to the blood on my arms and face that I had gotten from the branches earlier.

Lilith breathed in the air around her with her eyes closed and I took that as my opportunity to run to Ella who had just started to stir.

"So you're the son King Aldric claimed to be dead. I should have known he was lying that son of a bitch!" she sneered and turned to me. "I'll deal with him soon, don't you worry."

"What's going on?" Ella asked as she opened her eyes.

She looked around the room and shock covered her features as she saw Lilith. Then she saw Hulda and went to run over to her but I held her back.

"She better be okay or I swear..." Ella started.

"You swear what, witch? You haven't got what it takes. Your kind are all pathetic and weak." Lilith scoffed as she crossed her arms.

She sauntered towards the dining table and grabbed a chair, moving it next to Hulda and taking a seat. "Let's talk shall we?" Her lips turned up into an evil smirk.

"What do you want from me?" Ella asked.

"What do I want from you? Don't be so self absorbed, little witch. This has never been about you. This has been about your dear Hulda here. Has she never told you why I came to your house that night?"

"Don't listen to her, Ella. She's trying to get into your head," I whispered in her ear.

"What reason would I have to lie?" Lilith crossed her legs.

Hulda started to wake up. She looked beside her to see Lilith and flinched. Lilith laughed as she removed the gag from

249

Hulda's mouth.

"What's going on? Why are you here?" Hulda asked Lilith, frantic.

"Perfect timing. You're awake and I was about to tell your daughter-like witch here why I came to her house all those years ago and killed her parents," Lilith smirked. "Or did you want the honour?"

"Hulda, what is she talking about?" Ella asked cautiously.

"Don't do this, Lilith. Your quarrel is with me and me alone. Leave Ella out of this." Hulda ignored Ella's question.

"Fine. I'll tell her." Lilith clicked her tongue.

"Ella, please. I was going to tell you. I just couldn't find the right time." Hulda was sobbing now.

"Oh for goodness sake, get yourself together, Hulda," Lilith said, getting to her feet. "Did Hulda ever tell you what she was running from the night your parents took her in?"

Ella looked from Lilith to Hulda. "No... she didn't."

"Her father was the leader of their coven and tried to sum-mon me to gain more power for them all. Silly old man thinking he can demand such a thing from the Demon Queen," she tsked. "I agreed on the condition that he hand over his daughter to me."

"Hand over Hulda?" I asked.

"Yes, Fenris. Do keep up. I'm surprised you are my own flesh and blood," Lilith spat.

I flinched at the hatred in her words, the venom. I was her son, she had just learnt this information and she didn't care whatsoever. I wished I could say that it didn't hurt, but it did. I loathed the Demon Queen, I wanted nothing more than to see her dead, and yet, I found myself also yearning for that motherly connection. I knew it was fruitless, because I would never get it from someone like her.

"Her father agreed to a blood oath. Stupid, pathetic mortal." Lilith rolled her eyes.

"What did you do to him?" I questioned.

Lilith inspected her claws. "Oh, you know, I turned him into a monster and let him loose on his own coven. I gave him what he wanted, more power. He wasn't specific enough about what exactly he was after." She grinned. "The blood bath was truly delightful! Unfortunately, Hulda here was able to escape and she made her way right to your doorstep, witch." Lilith pointed at Ella.

"Please, stop," Hulda cried out.

Lilith ignored her. "She had no idea I was following her the whole time." She laughed. "She screamed the whole forest down for help until your parents lowered their wards, revealing their home, this home."

"So, my parents didn't do anything wrong?" Ella asked, a tear escaping down her cheek. I held her tighter.

"They got in my way. That in itself is enough of a crime to warrant their immediate deaths." Lilith rolled her shoulders. "I killed your parents because I wanted to. Your father pleaded for his life and your mother's life, you know? It was thrilling when I struck him down, his eyes were still wide open as he hit the forest floor. I watched your mother try to flee through the trees when I threw my power right at her back and watched her fall to the ground, crawling away to die." Lilith laughed. "I left and came back when my energy was replenished to find an abandoned cottage." Lilith pointed to Hulda. "I assume that was your doing? A little warding to make me think you had moved on?"

I could feel Ella tense beneath my arms. It was taking

everything in her not to strike at Lilith right now, I don't know how she had the strength to stand her ground.

Hulda smiled nervously. "It fooled you didn't it?"

Lilith struck Hulda against the cheek with her claws, leaving three bloody scratches.

"Stop, leave her alone." Ella tried to break free of my grasp, but I still wouldn't let her go.

I knew eventually I'd have to, but right now I needed to hold her.

"How did you know to come back now then?" I asked.

"My demons informed me of a witch that was causing havoc. Killed a Scree Demon and was after more demon blood. My demons are everywhere and report back to me. One of them followed you home one day, Ella. Watched you kill another demon with your little Witch Hunter here. When he saw Hulda he came straight back to me and told me."

"Just take me and leave Ella alone. I'm the one that was promised to you." Hulda was calmer now.

"Well, I need to teach you a lesson don't I? Not to run from me. I also need to teach young Ella here a lesson. That she can't go killing my demons and get away with it," Lilith snarled. "I also recall a fortune teller once informing me that a witch and Witch Hunter would be my undoing. Seems a bit coincidental being here in this moment, doesn't it? Best I take you all out before you take me out."

"I won't let you hurt her," I said, standing up and pulling Ella up with me.

"What a gentleman my son appears to be. We'll have to change that. For now, I will be killing Ella and I will be imprisoning Hulda. I'll decide your fate after." Her voice was like a stab to the chest, no care, no stutter, just pure evil.

"I said... I won't let you hurt her." I unsheathed the Sword of Fatum and Lilith's red eyes widened.

"How did you get that?" she sneered.

"Brackas says hi." I smirked.

CHAPTER 28

MARELLA

"Fenris, no!" I yelled, trying to hold him back but he slipped from my grasp.

He moved towards Lilith, the Sword of Fatum almost glowing with energy.

Lilith held up her hand towards Hulda and as she did, Hulda's restraints were loosened and she disappeared, reappearing right in front of Lilith.

Fenris came to a halt, managing to stop in time to avoid driving the sword through Hulda. Lilith laughed and threw Fenris against a wall with the flick of her arm. I ran towards him and helped him to his feet.

Lilith shoved Hulda against the wall hard, she collapsed in a heap on the floor.

"Give me the sword and I will spare all of you," Lilith roared.

I looked at Fenris who looked at me and I shook my head. If we gave her the sword she would kill us anyway and then go on to destroy the world. It was destiny, after all.

Fenris twirled the hilt of the sword in his hand. "Seems your sister wasn't as good a guardian as you imagined."

"What did you do?" Lilith's eyes glowed red.

"She's dead, but don't worry, Brackas is still very much alive."

Lilith hissed and lunged at us but Fenris pushed me out of the way, tackling her, the Sword of Fatum clanking as it fell from his hand and hit the ground.

Fenris was holding her down, his lips turned up into a snarl. I had never seen him so hateful before.

My fire was itching at my palms, to hurl it at Lilith, but I held myself back. This was Fen's fight, but I also didn't have a clear shot of her anyway. I couldn't risk hitting him.

Lilith broke free and got to her feet.

"HOW DARE YOU!" she screamed.

Fenris grabbed the Sword of Fatum from the ground and pulled his dagger from his belt, standing in front of me.

Lilith flung her arm towards Fenris, but as she did he held up his runed dagger. A bright white light filled the entire cottage. Lilith shrank back, but righted herself almost immediately.

"Nice trick, but do you really think it can stop me for long?" she hissed.

"No harm in trying." Fenris' eyes stared at her and his lips thinned.

"Fenris, I will only give you this option once because you're my blood. Get out of my way so I can kill your witch or so help me I'll kill you with her," Lilith snarled, the desperation laced in her tone.

255

"You can have me just leave him alone," I said.

I turned to Fenris "Promise me you'll protect Hulda?" I asked.

"No, I won't let you," he answered.

"You promised, Fen. Let me do this."

Lilith tapped her heel on the ground. "What will it be? I will kill you all if I have to... even you Fenris."

He looked into my eyes. "I can't. I'm sorry."

Fenris turned and ran at Lilith, the Sword of Fatum in his grasp when Lilith summoned her own sword in her hands and threw it.

There was a clank as the Sword of Fatum fell to the floor and Fenris threw himself in front of me. This wasn't part of *my* vision. I thought it was me who was destined to die, but I realised my vision had ended before the sword ever landed.

The sword plunged straight into Fenris' chest. He stumbled before falling to his knees, grasping the sword in his hands. I fell to the ground next to him, hands fluttering uselessly at the sword buried in his chest.

His breathing was bubbly and wet. Tears burned my eyes and escaped down my cheeks, falling over his face. I pulled him into my lap as I heard Lilith laugh.

"Fenris, no. Please don't leave me. Stay with me," I pleaded.

He slumped backwards into my lap. His eyes began to flutter as I brushed his hair with my fingers.

"I love you, Ella," he whispered through his shallow breathing.

"Fenris, I love you. Please, I love you. Stay. Don't... don't go." My heart struck me with pain.

He took one last gasp before closing his eyes, his body going limp in my arms.

Fenris' body started to disappear in my arms until I was holding nothing.

"Where is he? What have you done with him?" I screamed as I looked at Lilith.

Hatred blazed through my tears and I glared at her. She smiled evilly back down at me.

"I hate you!" I screamed.

She opened her smirking mouth, but no words came out. Instead, she jerked violently, her eyes bulging with terror as she clutched at her chest. Where a blade protruded, dripping with her black blood. But it wasn't just any blade, it was the Sword of Fatum.

From behind her, Hulda released the hilt, staggering away.

Lilith's body disappeared, a look of shock and despair on her face, and the sword dropped to the ground, turning to ash right before our eyes.

"He's gone." I walked over to Hulda and sobbed into her shoulder.

She wrapped her arms around me and I felt her shake. "Ella, I'm so sorry. For everything. For your parent's death and not telling you the truth."

I removed my head from her shoulder. "Not now, Hulda. I can't do this right now. He's gone. Fenris is …"

Losing Fenris was the worst pain I had ever gone through. Every heartbeat without him was like a dagger to my soul. How could I recover from this? I loved him. He loved me. It was supposed to be me who died, not him! It's all my fault he's gone.

"Wait…" I said as I looked at Hulda. "Higher demons don't die. They go back to Hell."

"I'm not sure what you mean, honey." Hulda looked on with

concern.

"Fenris is Lilith's son. He would be a higher demon." I walked towards the spot where he had taken his last breath. "He's in Hell. He has to be. I won't accept anything else."

"Oh sweetie, he may not be," Hulda said, brushing her hand through my hair.

"He is!" I stood, wiping the tears and blood from my face, baring my teeth in a feral snarl at Hulda. "I know it. And I'm going to get him back."

EPILOGUE

FENRIS

I opened my eyes and was faced with pitch black darkness. I held up my hands but I couldn't even see them in front of me. I couldn't see anything. Where was I?

"Ella," I whispered.

Nothing. I was alone.

I focused on what I could hear and feel. Slowly shuffling to the left I eventually hit a wall.

It felt as though it was made of cool stone. It was freezing, I realised. Although I couldn't see the goosebumps on my skin I knew they were there, I could feel them. My body was wracked with chills.

I could hear the dripping sound of water close by. My mouth was dry and begging for a taste. I could just make out a clanging noise. I had no idea what it was or where it was coming from, but it was a distant sound.

A sudden, bloodcurdling scream pierced my ears and made me stumble back and shrink into the wall. Where was I? I heard another scream and flinched. This couldn't be good. I had to get out of here somehow.

What was the last thing I remembered? I hit my palms to my head. Think, Fenris, think. What happened right before I woke up.

It came to me. Lilith. She had killed me with her sword. So how was I alive? Or was I dead? Is this what death felt like? Surely not. I was a good person. I did my duty to my kingdom and served my King... my father, I guess. That had to mean if I were to die I'd end up somewhere nicer than this.

Unless I was in... no, it can't be. Please no. There was no way I was in Hell. I couldn't accept something so horrid.

In the distance, a faint, blinking light moved. It was coming closer. As it approached I realised it was a flaming torch, and my surroundings appeared from out of the darkness.

I was in a prison. The prison was made of stone, as I suspected, and housed a dirty old mattress on the ground and a bucket in the corner that I assumed was for toilet matters. The bars in front of me were made out of hard, thick steel. The space itself was so small, and I could just make out other cells around my own. Why was I here? How was I here?

I needed to figure out a way to escape. To get back to Ella and make sure she was okay. I had no idea how I'd even begin to get out of this place but there had to be a way.

The torch got closer and I could make out two people's silhouettes but I couldn't see their faces behind the light that was now so bright it was hurting my eyes. I had no idea how long I'd been down here for, how long I'd been left unconscious for. My eyes were no longer accustomed to the light. I rubbed them and watched as the figure holding the torch moved it away so I could see their face.

"Hello, son. Are you ready to become one of us?"

ACKNOWLEDGMENTS

I want to thank everyone that made this book possible. I wouldn't be here, publishing this book, if it wasn't for all of you.

To my husband, Luke and my daughter, Alice. You have both been so incredible and patient with me while I worked tirelessly to pump this book out. I am so thankful that Luke helped frame the story into what it is.

To my wonderful best friend, Emma. I have no idea what I would have done without you. Alpha reading, beta reading and editing my work. I'd be lost without you. You've been my rock and I lobe you (not a typo). Also, you can all thank Emma for chapter 18. IYKYK. She begged for a spicy scene when she saw red satin sheets so I gave her one.

To Layla Pine, one of my good friends and also one of my absolute favourite authors of all time (seriously, go read her books). Thank you so much for alpha reading my work. Thank you for being there for me. You're a literal gem.

To all my beta readers, thank you so much for taking the time to read Echoes of Fate and leave your suggestions. You all have helped me so much.

To all my arc readers, you are all superstars! Thank you to the moon and back.

To my mother, Norma. You have always encouraged us to follow our dreams. You have nurtured our creative side and been our biggest cheerleader. You're a beautiful human being and the most incredible mother.

Thank you to the members of the Facebook group I co own. Australian and New Zealand Book Lovers. You have all been so incredibly supportive of me and I can't thank you all enough.

And thank you to everyone who purchases and reads my book. Your support means the absolute world to me. I've worked so hard to get this book as close to perfect as I can so to have you all support me is just so beautiful.

Milton Keynes UK
Ingram Content Group UK Ltd.
UKHW031120261124
451585UK00004B/375

9 781763 790704